D1584826

Teasing the Tiger

RAYNA TYLER

Copyright © 2020 Rayna Tyler

All rights reserved. No part of this publication may be reproduced, stored in a retrieval system, or transmitted, in any form or by any means, without the prior written permission of the author.

This is a work of fiction. Names, characters, places, and incidents are either the product of the author's imagination or are used fictitiously, and any resemblance to actual persons living or dead, business establishments, events, or locales, is entirely coincidental.

ISBN: 978-1-953213-09-9

ALSO BY RAYNA TYLER

Seneca Falls Shifters

Tempting the Wild Wolf
Captivated by the Cougar
Enchanting the Bear
Enticing the Wolf
Teasing the Tiger

Ketaurran Warriors

Jardun's Embrace
Khyron's Claim
Zaedon's Kiss
Rygael's Reward
Logan's Allure

Crescent Canyon Shifters

Engaging His Mate
Impressing His Mate

CHAPTER ONE

MITCH

"Are you telling me I drove all the way over here because you thought you saw a tiger in your backyard?" Seeing a wolf, even a bear, wouldn't have surprised me, but a jungle cat was hard to imagine.

"That was your emergency?" I scrubbed a hand over my face after giving Alma Chapman a skeptical glance, then peered again through the double-paned glass of the patio door at the animal-free forest behind her property.

Until now, being confused was not a description I would've used to describe the elderly woman who had to be pushing eighty years old. She was a retired grade school teacher and one of my longtime customers. Or I should say, Trixie, her black-and-gray-striped cat, was one of my patients. The animal was currently perched on the back of a nearby sofa, licking her front paw, seemingly unaware of her owner's concerns.

Since I was the only vet with a home in the Colorado mountain area near the town of Ashbury, dealing with pet emergencies came with the territory. Though I was pretty sure catching imaginary tigers went way beyond anything listed in my job description.

"Don't give me that look, Mitchell Jacobson." She waggled her bony index finger at me. "I know what you're thinking, and I am *not* senile. I know what I saw."

All my friends and family, except for my mother when she was angry, called me Mitch. Alma, from the first time I'd met her, insisted on using the formal name I'd been given at birth. Tacking on the last name was her way of telling me she meant business.

I searched for a compliment, hoping it would distract her. "Those are nice glasses. Are they new?" I'd grasped at the first thing I could think of, which turned out to be a mistake.

"I'm not blind either." She harrumphed and pushed the thick wire-rimmed bifocals farther up her nose.

While I stood there trying to figure out the best way to remove myself from her home without upsetting her further, I caught a streak of black and orange out of my periphery. I looked outside just in time to see the not so imaginary animal disappear through a gap in the trees. I shook my head. "Well, I'll be darned."

Alma crossed her arms and jutted out her chin. "I told you I saw a tiger out there."

A few seconds later, the cat reappeared. It was a beautiful creature, and I found myself more fascinated than afraid. The animal skidded to a stop near a patch of wildflowers, then pressed its nose against the white and purple blossoms. After a couple of sniffs, it jostled its head and sneezed before playfully bounding after a butterfly.

"Did you see that?" Alma took off her glasses and used the bottom of her shirt to clean the lenses, then slipped them back into place. "Is that normal behavior for a wild animal?"

"I have no idea." I wasn't an expert on predatory cats. The only tigers I'd ever been this close to were ones I'd seen at the zoo in California, and that had been back when I was a teenager. I certainly didn't recall any of them sniffing flowers or chasing butterflies.

Some of the families that lived nearby had children and small pets. Letting the animal continue to roam the area put their lives in danger. I slipped my cell phone out of my back pants pocket, then ran my thumb through my contacts list.

Alma placed her hand on my arm. "What are you doing?"

"I'm going to call the park rangers. They're better equipped to deal with this kind of situation." Some of the nearby land was part of a national forest, and the rangers had a station located in the area.

"You can't," she gasped. "The resort's property borders mine. What if, you know,"—she leaned closer to whisper, as if the room was filled with other people who might overhear her—"the tiger is one of their special guests?"

Special guests. It didn't take me long to realize what Alma was referring to. The Seneca Falls Resort was owned by a family of shifters, wolves, to be exact. Quite a few of their guests had the ability to transform into animals, a fact the shifter community rarely shared with humans. I was under the impression I was one of the few non-shifting people in the area who even knew they existed. "Alma, I'm sure I have no…"

She stopped me with a narrow-eyed glare, one I was sure she'd used regularly on her past students. "You've been friends with Reese, Berkley, and Nick for a long time. Don't pretend you don't know they're wolves." She harrumphed at me again. "Or that Bryson, the sweet boy your sister Leah married, isn't a bear."

"How did you find out?" My friends and my sister's mate took extra precautions to protect their animal sides, and they wouldn't have shared the information with Alma, not unless she'd been in a life-threatening situation. Berkley and her brothers had even designed a secluded area on their property for shifters so they could let their animals run without being observed by any human guests.

Poachers used to be a big concern when they'd first inherited the resort, so they'd hired a security team to ensure everyone's safety. The area also had special signs posted on the trees designating the boundaries.

A wily grin spread across her face. "You don't get to be my age and live on this mountain as long as I have without finding out about other people's secrets."

"Okay, then." I shoved my phone back into my pocket. "What do you suggest we do about the tiger?"

"Can't you go out there and talk to it? Maybe give it directions back to the resort?" Alma asked.

I shot her a sidelong glare, half expecting her to produce a map of the area for me to use while giving the animal instructions. "Let's assume you're right about the tiger being a shifter." I continued to watch the animal's odd behavior. It had stopped chasing the butterfly and had risen up on its hind legs to get a drink from a concrete birdbath near the trees at the back of the yard.

"What if it doesn't like what I have to say, or sees me as a threat because I'm human, then decides to eat me instead?" I'd been hoping she had a better solution, one that didn't involve the possibility of bloodshed.

"Good point." Alma tapped her chin and crinkled her nose. "Aren't vets supposed to have guns that shoot darts to put animals to sleep?"

"If you mean a tranquilizer gun, then yes, I have one in my truck." I'd rarely had a reason to use the weapon, but still kept it stashed underneath the back seat, mostly as a precaution in case I ran into an animal causing problems. I'd never used it on a shifter and wasn't even sure if the darts were powerful enough to knock one out.

"Yes, one of those." She smiled. "You could shoot the tiger with a dart, then, once it's asleep, you can take it up to the lodge and ask them to look after it."

It might not be a great idea, but it wasn't a bad one either. The only part of the plan I intended to change, provided I didn't get mauled first, was to call Reese and confirm he had a tiger for a guest before taking the animal to the lodge. News traveled fast on the mountain, and the last thing my friends needed was unwanted publicity.

I wasn't totally convinced the animal was a shifter, especially since it was a long way from the resort's safety zone. If it truly was a tiger, I'd be justified in shooting it. If I was wrong, then I'd be doing quite a bit of apologizing to its human side once it woke up. If that was the case, I'd have to rely on Reese and Berkley to help smooth things over.

"Stay here and keep an eye on the tiger while I run out to my truck." I headed back through the living room, since I'd parked the vehicle on the gravel drive near the front of Alma's house. With any luck, the animal would stay in the backyard long enough for me to retrieve the gun and get back inside.

***

HANNAH

I propped my front paws on the edge of the birdbath and lapped some of the cool water. Shifting into my cat and taking a run had been a good idea. It cleared my mind and helped me work through the plot problems I was having with my latest mystery novel. Unfortunately, it also helped me realize that having the heroine find a dead body facedown in a koi fish pond wasn't going to work in the current chapter I was writing.

Rewriting a few thousand words was another delay I couldn't afford. My editor wasn't happy when she found out I might miss my deadline, and she'd been less than thrilled when I told her I had plans for a trip to stay at a Colorado lodge for a few days. I'd hoped leaving the city to enjoy the breathtaking mountain scenery would help inspire my muse so I could finish my book.

To be honest, I was beating myself up based on extremely high expectations. I'd arrived at the Seneca Falls Resort only a few hours ago, which wasn't nearly enough time to relax and work out my plot issues. I chuffed, then dropped to the ground and flexed my paws.

Being a highly creative person with a tendency to be completely drawn into my imaginary worlds, I sometimes forgot to pay attention to where I was going. Now that I was back to focusing on my surroundings, I thought it was strange that someone would put a birdbath in the middle of the forest. At least I did until I spotted a single-story home with a mustard-color finish and white trim at the opposite side of the clearing.

I glanced at the nearby trees and started to worry when I didn't see any of the wooden signs that marked the resort's area designated as a shifter run. Somehow, I'd left the protected zone and ended up in someone's backyard.

This was not good, nor was it the first time I'd gotten myself into this kind of predicament. Most shifters had an enhanced sense of smell, but mine was adequate. Having bad allergies only made it worse.

It was why whenever I traveled, I made sure to take my best friend, Sydney Jamison, with me. She was an arctic fox shifter, a wilderness guide by profession, and great at keeping me focused. If she hadn't been hired by a large corporation to accompany them on their two-week management team retreat, she'd be with me now. Since she was unreachable by cell and with my deadline quickly approaching, I'd decided to risk taking the trip alone.

A mistake I was certain I was going to pay for when I caught a glimpse of a female through the house's glass patio door. She stared at me through her glasses with the kind of expression I'd expect on someone who'd noticed bubblegum stuck in my fur.

Even more disconcerting was the way the gorgeous male with short, silky brown hair gazed at me with intense dark eyes. Our brief staring match ended with me making a growly gasp after he slid the door open and stepped onto the concrete patio holding a gun and aiming it in my direction.

I understood how seeing a tiger roaming around their backyard would be unsettling. I was adept at protecting myself, but since I was the one doing the trespassing, I couldn't blame him for wanting to shoot me.

On the other hand, if he managed to get in a good shot, I didn't want to end up as a rug in front of his fireplace. The muscles in my chest tightened, making my already ragged breathing more difficult.

I definitely didn't want to be shot. Even though shifting into my human form would have been the simplest way to keep that from happening, it wasn't an option, and neither was staying here. Our kind had strict rules about exposing ourselves to humans.

If I could scent worth a darn, I'd be able to determine which direction led back to the lodge. Since I couldn't do that either, I did what any sensible tiger who could easily outrun a human male would do. I ran back into the forest, staying close to the trees and any large bushes I could use for cover.

After a few minutes of glancing behind me and not seeing any sign of the male, I slowed to a walk. If I strayed too far from the area, I'd risk losing my way back to the resort altogether. Growing up without a decent sense of smell had forced me to develop other skills. I'd learned to mentally document important details when I wasn't paying attention.

Right now what I needed was a landmark, something I'd seen, something that would trigger my memory and help me find my way back to the lodge.

I hadn't gone far when another patch of wildflowers caught my attention. The purple flowers with yellow centers were exquisitely beautiful. I couldn't resist stopping to press my nose against the delicate blossoms, hoping to catch a whiff of their fragrance.

After three unsuccessful attempts to inhale even the slightest hint of their floral aroma, I shook my head and sneezed. One sneeze led to another, and by the time I was done, my eyes were watering.

It was depressing to think I might be the only tiger shifter on the entire planet with allergies so severe, I couldn't smell well enough to scent or track…anything.

A butterfly like the one I'd seen earlier caught my eye, and I changed direction to follow it. This one had brilliant black-veined orange wings. At first I thought it might be a monarch, but then decided it was more than likely a front range. The species had a similar appearance and was predominant in this area of Colorado. The only way I'd know for sure was by getting closer, and since I was never one to ignore my cat's curiosity, I romped along after it.

The insect flitted from one patch of blossoms to another. When it finally landed on a petal, I crouched on the ground and eased closer. I had almost reached the flower, was seconds away from getting my answer, when I felt a sharp pinch on my right flank.

I pushed to my paws, my startled growl more of a yelp. When I turned my head to see what had caused the pain, I found a dart sticking out of my fur. Sydney once told me my distractions were going to be the death of me. Of course, she'd been teasing at the time, but now I wondered if she'd been right.

In my quest to observe the butterfly, I'd forgotten all about the handsome male. He was standing fifteen or so feet away from me, with his gun still pointed at my rear. I could feel the effects of the drug rushing through my system and didn't have long to consider why he'd be frowning, not smiling about his well-aimed shot.

I tried to take a step, but my muscles refused to cooperate, and I stumbled. My legs wobbled, and I dropped to the ground. At least he hadn't killed me, but that didn't mean I wasn't going to wake up in a zoo or in a cage somewhere on another continent. I shuddered, the horrid thought the last thing racing through my mind before everything faded to darkness.

CHAPTER TWO

MITCH

As soon as the tiger moved away from the birdbath, I stepped onto the patio behind Alma's house. Surprisingly, the animal didn't growl or take a predatory stance. It simply sprinted into the woods. Following after it hadn't been the smartest thing to do, not if it decided to stalk me, to silently sneak up from behind and attack. Yet for some inexplicable reason, I was drawn to the beautiful feline. I cared about its welfare and didn't want the rangers anywhere near it.

When I finally caught up to the tiger, it was back to chasing a butterfly. The scrutiny it gave the small insect after it landed on the petals of a wildflower was baffling. The big cat seemed so preoccupied that it hadn't heard my approach, giving me plenty of time to aim without having to worry that I'd miss if it decided to move.

The instant the tiger snarled and dropped to the ground, I regretted pulling the trigger. What made it worse was seeing the shock in a pair of green eyes that appeared more human than feline.

I squatted next to the large cat and removed the dart.

"I'm so sorry." I ran my hand along its striped fur in a soothing motion while I pondered the best way to deal with it. My truck had four-wheel drive, so I could easily drive it into the woods without fear of getting stuck. My current problem was figuring out how I was going to lift a three-hundred-pound tiger into the bed of the vehicle, something I hadn't even considered until now.

About a year ago, I'd modified my home to include a small clinic with Saturday hours to save the residents on the mountain—of which there were quite a few—from having to drive to my main office in Ashbury. I'd also included a kennel in case I ended up with overnight patients. The two gated stalls were designed with large dogs in mind, but I was pretty sure one of them was big enough to accommodate a full-grown tiger.

The solid form beneath my hand vibrated, and the sound of popping and crackling filled the air. Startled, I jumped to my feet and stared in awe as the tiger's tail disappeared and its fur receded, replaced by smooth, creamy skin. In less than a minute, the cat had transformed into a woman.

Strawberry-blonde curls framed her face, and a light sprinkling of freckles covered her pert nose and rounded cheeks. Even though she lay on her side, it was hard not to notice her firmly toned body and the curve of her breasts not covered by the arm she draped across them.

"Oh, hell," I muttered and averted my gaze. Admiring a naked woman when it was her choice was one thing. Ogling her while she was unconscious was another. After setting the gun on the ground, I unbuttoned and removed my shirt.

My truck dilemma might have resolved itself, but now I was faced with a bigger problem—a female who was going to be extremely unhappy with me when she woke up.

I'd barely gotten my shirt draped over her chest and hips when I heard the sound of twigs snapping and dry leaves crunching. My pulse raced, and I spun around to find Alma walking toward me. "What happened to waiting in the house until I came back?"

She flicked her wrist. "You were taking too long." She glanced at the woman, a frown deepening her wrinkles. "Besides, I figured you might need this." She held out the blanket she had bundled in her arms.

"How did you know?"

"For a vet, you sure don't know much about shifters, do you?"

"Apparently not." I scowled, then snatched the blanket away from her. Every now and then, the shifters living in the area came to me to treat their injuries instead of going to the hospital in Hanford. I liked to stay up-to-date so I could treat them properly and planned to do a little research to find out if the tiger's transformation back into her human half had anything to do with her current drug-induced state.

I knelt beside the woman again and rolled her as I wrapped the blanket around her. With Alma hovering over me, I thought it was best not to worry about retrieving my shirt until later. After gently lifting her off the ground, I shifted her in my arms so her head leaned against my shoulder. She smelled like the wildflowers she'd been sniffing. Remembering the way her cat chased the butterflies brought a smile to my lips.

Alma drew me from my thoughts with a smack to the back of my head, much as I imagined she'd done with her son when he was a lot younger.

"What was that for?"

"Just in case you decide to do something stupid where that girl is concerned."

I was surprised at how hard Alma could hit, and would have rubbed my head if my hands weren't full. From what I'd seen of the shifter before I covered her with my shirt, she definitely wasn't a girl. She was a full-grown female, and a beautiful one at that. Not that I'd ever argue either point with Alma.

"Give me a little credit, will you?" I moved out of her reach and returned her glare. "I promise I'll take good care of her."

"See that you do." She headed back toward her home. Instead of going inside, she circled the side of the house and walked over to my truck. When she reached the passenger side, she opened the door and stepped aside.

"Thanks." I positioned the woman on the seat, then strapped her in with the belt.

"Mitchell," Alma said.

I closed the door, hoping there wasn't something else she'd forgotten to lecture me about. "Yes?"

"Will you call and let me know how the poor thing is doing?"

"I'd be happy to." Provided her cat didn't shred me to pieces after she woke up. I followed her as she circled around the front of my truck, then opened the driver's door while she headed toward her house. Alma stopped when she reached the porch.

"Oh, and I expect to get that blanket back when you're finished with it."

After Alma disappeared inside, I shook my head and got into the truck, then drove to the end of her gravel drive. After glancing at my sleeping passenger, I dismissed the idea of taking her to the resort, then turned right onto the two-lane road leading back to my place.

Even though things would go a lot smoother if Berkley was around when the female woke up, I didn't want to take her to the lodge until I knew for certain she was actually staying there. I didn't know who she was and had no personal attachment to her, but the thought of anyone, especially another male, taking care of her grated along my nerves.

I was the one who shot her, and until I found out more about her and where she came from, she was my responsibility. I also justified my decision by telling myself I needed to be there when she woke up so I could apologize profusely for what I now considered a poor use of judgment.

With a game plan in mind, I tapped the button for the phone on my steering wheel and gave it a voice command to call Berkley's cell phone rather than Reese's. For this particular situation, I figured she'd be a lot easier to deal with than her older brother.

"Hey, Mitch," she answered on the third ring, her voice pleasant and professional. "What's going on?"

I knew she had caller ID and always checked to see whose name was on the screen before accepting any calls. "Berkley." I wasn't looking forward to explaining what I'd done and took a deep breath. "I have a problem and could sure use your help."

***

HANNAH

My mind was filled with hazy images of pale purple wildflowers and orange butterflies. As my thoughts became clearer, my head ached and I could feel a dull pain near my right hip. I remembered landing on the ground, but couldn't recall why the dirt would feel so warm and soft.

I forced one eye open, then the other, expecting to find myself lying on a bed of dead leaves and pine needles. Not on a firm yet comfortable four-poster bed. At first I thought I might be dreaming and blinked my eyes several times to be sure. The unfamiliar bed didn't disappear, nor did the navy-blue comforter covering my completely naked body.

This bedroom was larger than the one in the cabin I'd rented at the resort. Filling one wall was a full-length dresser and mirror, the wood tone a medium shade of maple. Centered on the adjacent wall was a matching armoire that completed the bedroom set.

I was surrounded by scents I didn't recognize, the most prominent one belonging to a human male. I slowly turned my head to sniff the fluffy pillow. From what I could smell, my cat and I agreed the male was all kinds of enticing, which had me snuggling the material a lot longer than I should have.

Wonderful smell aside, the thought of not knowing where I was or how I'd gotten there was more than a little unsettling. It was all the motivation I needed to roll onto my side and try to get out of bed. Too bad my body wasn't willing to cooperate. I'd made it into a semi-sitting position before my throbbing head and nauseous stomach put an end to any thought of escape. I wasn't even sure if I could muster enough energy to shift. Not being able to transform into my tiger left me feeling vulnerable, which in turn jump-started my overactive imagination, one of the byproducts of being a mystery writer.

All sorts of what-if scenarios began flooding my mind. Like what if I'd been kidnapped and my captor planned to sell me to the circus? What if there was a private zoo out there that specialized in displaying shifters? Or what if one of my overzealous fans, like that woman who'd started a club of one and stalked me on a regular basis, had tracked me down and was keeping me prisoner?

My unrelenting speculations about why I was in a strange bed were brought to a halt by a knock on the door. I gasped and pulled the comforter up to my chin. The door opened, and a male poked his head inside. He looked familiar, I was certain I'd seen those dark brown eyes before, but seemed to be having a hard time reconciling where.

"Oh good, you're awake." He pushed the door open a little farther. "Do you mind if I come in?" His deep voice rolled across my skin in a wave of warmth that even had my cat taking an interest. My animal had great instincts when it came to judging someone's character, but she'd never perked her ears and flicked her tail this eagerly around a male before.

With my allergies impeding my ability to smell him from this distance, I could only assume he was the human male whose scent I'd gleaned from the pillow. "Um, okay." I'd never been kidnapped before, but all the research I'd done on the topic never mentioned the abductors being polite, so I decided it was okay to eliminate that possibility from my list.

Since he hadn't chained me to the bed and wasn't carrying any weapons, I figured he might not be a serial killer either. Telling him no didn't seem like a good choice, not if I wanted to find out why I was here. Not to mention the house probably belonged to him and he had every right to enter any room he wanted.

"Would you mind telling me who you are and where I'm at?"

"Mitch," he said, his half smile filled with trepidation. "My name is Mitch Jacobson, and you're in my home." He raised a brow, clearly expecting me to reciprocate.

"I'm Hannah." I wasn't about to tell him my last name, at least not until I got all my questions answered.

"It's nice to meet you, Hannah." He stepped into the room slowly, as if he was afraid he might spook me.

I tried not to giggle. I was part tiger, and the thought of him being able to scare me made me want to giggle. Instead, I took my time admiring his features: a tall frame, broad chest, and neatly groomed hairstyle. Judging by his button-down shirt and black slacks, I'd say he was some kind of professional who worked in an office. Though the tanned cheeks and blond highlights in his brown hair was a good indication he enjoyed spending time outside.

"How are you feeling?" He took a few more steps.

"I'm…" When he stopped a foot away from the bed, the parts of my memory that had been a little foggy snapped into place. I remembered where I'd seen him before and cringed. "You're the one who"—I rolled onto my side, pushing the blanket away so I could examine my hip—"shot me." Even with my enhanced healing abilities, the tiny red spot on the skin below my hip was still sore to the touch.

I jerked my head and pinned him with a glare. "Who are you, and why did you shoot me?" When I caught him staring at my exposed backside, I frowned and flipped the blanket back into place. I'd been in my tiger form when he'd pulled the trigger, which meant he'd seen me change into my human form. It also meant he'd put me in this bed, and he'd seen me completely naked.

I wasn't exactly happy about the being-seen-naked thing, but it was understandable, forgivable even, considering he'd made sure I was covered afterward. But letting a human find out shifters existed was a very big no-no in my world. All of a sudden, I couldn't breathe. I squeaked and clawed at my throat. No matter how much I gasped, I couldn't get any air into my lungs. I didn't get panic attacks often, but when I did, they also affected my cat, which unfortunately made shifting to protect myself impossible.

"It's okay." He held out his hands and sat on the edge of the bed next to me. "Try to take slow breaths."

I frowned and gulped more air that wasn't making it all the way into my lungs. "What the heck"—I gasped again—"do you think I'm trying to do?"

"Hey, look at me." He gently yet firmly clasped my chin.

I held his concerned gaze, but it wasn't helping.

The next thing I knew, his warm lips were covering mine. Somewhere in the back of my mind, the rational side was muttering that I should be offended, should be fighting to get away from him. I ignored the annoying warning and melted into his kiss. A gentle kiss that tingled and miraculously eased my anxiety. My breathing slowed, my lungs filled with air, and I was pretty sure I'd even done some moaning.

"Better?" he asked when he released me.

I'd been so distracted by the kiss that the blanket had slipped, displaying more of my breasts than I was comfortable sharing. I tucked the material under my arms to keep it in place, then set my hands in my lap. Even though I'd never met him before, and I knew it sounded crazy, there was something familiar about him. Something I should know, yet couldn't quite grasp.

Rather than cause myself further frustration, I forced my thoughts to move on to other topics, such as whether he planned to take advantage of me, and if he did, was I going to mind? "Why did you do that?"

"Because you were hyperventilating, and I didn't have a paper bag handy." His grin had my insides warming all the way to my toes.

I pursed my lips, ignoring the flutter in my stomach. "I was hyperventilating because you *shot* me."

"I'm really sorry about that." He swiped his hand along the side of his head, mussing some of the strands. "If I'd known you were a shifter, I wouldn't have… It's just that you're a tiger, and I've never seen one on the mountain before."

"About that." I could feel the heat rushing to my cheeks. "How do you know about our kind, and why aren't you afraid?" I'd heard there were humans who knew about us, but I'd never actually met one. I could only imagine how shocked someone would be at the discovery.

"My sister, Leah, is mated to a bear."

"Oh." I absently smoothed a wrinkle in the comforter.

"Do you mind if I ask how you ended up in Alma's backyard?"

"Is Alma the older female I saw you with before you…"

"Shot you, yeah." His wince seemed genuine.

"I'm not exactly sure." I tapped my chin. "I'd decided to go for a run to clear my head, and I thought I was doing okay because the area was marked with all these neat signs. The next thing I knew, I was sniffing flowers in your friend's backyard, and you know the rest."

"I take it you're staying at the resort?"

I nodded. "I arrived this morning. Or I think it was today, depending on how long I've been out." I'd been pretty groggy when I woke up and hated to think I'd lost more than a day.

"You were only out a couple of hours."

I blew out a relieved sigh. "Well, that's not so bad, then."

"I'm a little curious," he said.

"About what?"

"Why didn't you track your way back to the lodge?" He tapped the side of his nose, which I assumed was his way of referring to a shifter's enhanced smelling ability.

"Promise not to laugh?" Talking about my sniffing problem was embarrassing, not something I liked to share with anyone. If he hadn't seemed so concerned, been great about putting me at ease and helping me with my panic attack, I might not have been willing to tell him.

"I promise." His lopsided grin was adorable.

"I have bad allergies, and I can rarely get a decent scent." He didn't need to know that I also got distracted easily.

"Isn't that unusual for a shifter?" I couldn't detect any judgment in his tone, only curiosity. It was an endearing quality, one that impressed me.

"Yeah," I groaned. "Pretty much unheard of, at least in my family, anyway." My father accepted me the way I was, smelling problem and all. My mother, on the other hand, continually told her friends I was born with a handicap. I was pretty sure she would have told them I was adopted if she thought she could get away with it.

"If you're feeling better and would like to get back to the lodge, I'd be happy to drive you." He pushed off the bed. "It's the least I can do after ruining your day."

"Being shot wouldn't have been my choice of method, but it kept me out of trouble and from getting lost," I said, hoping to relieve some of his guilt since it didn't appear as if he was going to forgive himself anytime soon for what happened. "And a ride would be great."

I went to slide out of bed, then remembered I was naked. "Do you mind if I borrow your comforter?"

He chuckled, then walked over to a four-drawer dresser. "I think we can do a little better than that." He pulled out a T-shirt and a pair of sweatpants. "They're a little big, but they should keep you covered until we get back to the lodge." He set them on the bed, then hitched his thumb toward the door. "I'll wait for you outside."

"Thanks, but you can stay if you turn around." Maybe the drug was still causing side effects, because I couldn't explain why neither my cat nor I wanted him to leave.

"I can do that," he said, quickly turning to give me privacy.

It was more than likely my imagination, but I thought he'd sounded happy to comply, as if he hadn't wanted to leave the room either.

After grabbing the clothes, I slipped off the opposite side of the bed, then quickly tugged on the sweats and pulled the drawstring tight to keep them on my waist. I slipped the baggy T-shirt over my head, then plopped on the edge of the bed again so I could roll up the end of one pant leg. "You can turn around now." I finished adjusting the other leg and walked toward him.

He perused my attire from top to bottom. "I have to admit that shirt looks a lot better on you than it ever did on me."

I looked down to where the hem hit me midthigh, then rolled my eyes. "Uh-huh."

"Not to change the subject, but I was thinking about your allergy problem. I have a friend who works in the research department at the hospital over in Hanford. If you want, I could ask him if he's ever heard about the condition and see if they've developed anything that might help."

He was being so nice that I didn't have the heart to tell him I'd been to a specialist before and didn't have any luck. I guessed it wouldn't hurt to hear what his friend had to say. "If you're sure it's not any trouble." I didn't want to get my hopes up, but I would do almost anything to find a cure, to breathe normally again.

"It's no problem at all. Besides, it's a good cause and would make me feel better about having, you know..." He glanced at my backside.

"Well, I guess it's okay if it'll help ease your conscience." I smiled.

"Shall we?" He motioned me toward the open doorway, then urged me along the hallway to the right. "There is one more thing I meant to ask you."

"Only one?" I teased, then glanced in the two rooms we passed. One was another bedroom; the other had been turned into an office.

He laughed. "Okay, maybe a few."

"Feel free to ask as many as you like," I said when he hesitated.

"Why was your cat chasing butterflies? I would have thought she'd rather be hunting small animals like squirrels or rabbits."

"How could you think I would ever hurt something so cute and fluffy?" I was appalled by his assumption and could feel the heat rising on my cheeks.

He quirked a brow. "Seriously?"

Tigers were predators, so of course he'd assume I enjoyed eating smaller creatures. "Sorry, I'm kind of a vegetarian. Have been ever since I was little." It was one of many items on a list of things my mother didn't approve of.

"When you say kind of, does that include cooked meats as well?"

"Some, not all, but mostly anything with fur stays off the menu." He stopped in front of a closed door at the end of the hall. "My truck is parked outside the clinic." He turned the handle.

My steps faltered as images of being strapped to an exam table next to a counter filled with sharp instruments flashed through my mind. Had his kindness been an act? Had I misjudged him and been too hasty in crossing "serial killer" from my list? "Clinic?" I rasped through a constricting throat, hoping I wasn't about to have another panic attack.

"I'm a vet." He took my elbow and urged me into a reception area. "My main office is in Ashbury, but I opened a smaller one in my home to accommodate my neighbors. It was either that or have them continue showing up at all hours."

"That explains the dart gun." I released a nervous laugh.

Mitch unlocked the glass door leading outside. He glanced at my feet and frowned. "I'm afraid I don't have any shoes that will fit you."

"It's all right. I don't mind going barefoot."

"Well, I do." He whisked me off my feet.

I squeaked and wrapped my arms around his neck. "Do all your patients get this kind of special treatment?"

He headed toward the silver Ford truck parked on the graveled drive. "Only the cute ones who can shift into tigers."

CHAPTER THREE

MITCH

Apparently, Hannah's roaming had taken her close to several of the resort's neighbors before she'd ended up in Alma's backyard. Evan Cleary, a ranger who worked on the park lands surrounding Seneca Falls, had arrived at the lodge shortly after I'd dropped Hannah off at her cabin.

He was human, had no idea shifters existed, and wouldn't hesitate to capture Hannah if he'd caught her in her tiger form, unlike his shifter coworkers, who would have given Reese, Berkley, and Nick a warning about making sure their guests didn't stray, then filed a report dismissing the handful of sightings as false complaints.

Evan tucked his right thumb under the edge of his utility belt. "As I was saying, there've been some poachers reported in the area again, but I thought you'd want to know we got several calls this morning from people who thought they'd seen a tiger."

I leaned against one of the counters in the private kitchen used by the lodge's owners and staff, keeping my emotions masked as I pretended I had no idea what the male was talking about.

When James Reynolds built the resort he'd left to his grandchildren, he'd had the foresight to add an additional area to the lodge for the owners and employees. There was a kitchen area and a handful of bedrooms, each containing their own bathrooms.

Currently, only two of the bedrooms were occupied. One by Berkley and her mate, Preston, the other by Reese and his mate, Jac. Their half brother Nick recently built a new home not far from the lodge that he shared with his human mate, Mandy.

Reese stood next to me, arms crossed, calmly listening to Evan. If he was troubled by what the ranger had to say, he didn't show it. The male was good at concealing his emotions, a trait I assumed he'd developed during his tour in the military.

"A tiger, really?" Berkley scoffed, not nearly as reserved with her opinions as her brother. She shot a conspiratorial glance at Jac and Mandy, who were sitting across from her at a long rectangular table centered on one half of the room. There was no mistaking she was related to Reese. Her facial features were similar, with the same defined cheekbones and dark hair intermingled with several lighter shades of brown.

Mandy adjusted the strap of her overalls, the outfit she usually wore whenever she worked on the old building's plumbing. "Are you sure the report wasn't a hoax?" she asked, following her best friend's lead.

During the drive to the lodge, I'd called Berkley to let her know I was returning Hannah. She'd told me she'd gotten a call from Gabe Miller, a nearby neighbor who ran trail rides, letting her know that Evan was in the area and to be prepared in case I ran into him. Once I'd reached the lodge and seen the ranger's truck parked out front, I'd taken a side road and dropped Hannah off at her cabin, then extended Berkley's invitation for her to join us as soon as she'd changed her clothes.

Prior to my arrival, Berkley had informed the people in

the room about Hannah being the tiger the ranger was referring to. As far as I knew, she'd left out the part about me shooting Hannah with a tranquilizer dart. At least I hoped she had.

The great thing about being accepted as part of a family of shifters was the way they all pulled together when someone needed protecting. And right now, that someone was Hannah. The last thing they wanted or needed was anyone, most specifically a ranger who knew nothing about their kind, searching their property.

Hannah and I had only spent a short amount of time together, yet I couldn't help feeling more than a little protective of her myself. I planned to do everything possible to keep anything bad from happening to her. After hearing Evan tell us he was following up on the report, the guilt I felt over shooting Hannah lessened, and I was glad I'd gotten to her first.

"That's what we're trying to determine." Evan rubbed his clean-shaven chin. "And since one of the sightings wasn't far from here, I thought I'd stop by and give you a heads-up."

"We appreciate you taking the time to let us know." Reese pushed away from the counter and circled around the table, urging Evan toward the hallway outside the kitchen.

I waited until their footsteps faded and I was certain they were out of earshot before speaking to Berkley. "Is this going to cause you any problems?"

"We should be okay," she said. "Preston already talked to his security team, and they'll make sure none of the human rangers do any snooping around."

Berkley's mate was a cougar. He'd been friends with Reese ever since their time in the military and was now the resort's head of security.

"I'll need to have a talk with Hannah, though." Berkley's frown said it wasn't a conversation she was looking forward to. "We can't have her putting the rest of our nonhuman guests at risk."

I wanted to defend Hannah, to tell my friends what happened wasn't her fault, that there was a reason her cat had strayed. Information about her allergy problem had been shared in confidence, and I didn't think it was my place to tell anyone else about it. Though I was sure if they knew, they'd be a lot more understanding about the situation.

Footsteps too light to be Reese's echoed from the hallway. Bear, Nick and Mandy's dog, whimpered from the spot under the kitchen table where he'd been sleeping. He was a mutt, not much bigger than a fox terrier. If he'd viewed whoever was approaching as a threat, he'd be on his feet and growling instead of swishing his brown tail back and forth.

"Excuse me, but the female working at the reception desk said it was okay to come back." The woman standing in the doorway sounded a lot like Hannah. She wore dark glasses and had blonde hair, which, after closer scrutiny, I realized had to be a wig.

"Hannah, is that you?" I asked, walking toward her and wondering if she'd overheard anything Berkley had said.

"Yeah." She slipped off the glasses.

"Oh, my gosh, you look so familiar." Mandy's blue eyes widened, and she snapped her fingers. "You're Hannah Lawrence, aren't you?"

"The famous mystery writer?" Jac had her back to the doorway and had strained her neck to get a better look at Hannah.

"Yes." Mandy was practically bouncing up and down in her seat.

"I don't know about famous, but I do write mysteries." Hannah smiled, the freckles on her cheeks highlighted by her blush.

Mandy nudged Berkley's arm. "Why didn't you tell us she was staying here?"

Berkley shot Mandy a sidelong glare. "Maybe because

my guests have a right to their privacy." She smiled at Hannah. "Besides, the last name on the registration says Walker, not Lawrence."

"Lawrence is my pen name," Hannah said.

"See?" Berkley sneered.

Mandy shook her head at her friend. "Even if she'd used her pen name, you wouldn't have known who she was. Admit it."

"Didn't they let you do any recreational reading while you were away at that fancy college?" Jac asked.

Berkley narrowed her brown eyes and snorted. "Unlike others, who were gallivanting around the world with their camera, I was actually trying to get a degree in marketing." She tapped her nails on the table. "Although, I did enjoy the class on how to skin a cat. Would you like a demonstration?"

Jac playfully hissed at Berkley, drawing a giggle from Hannah. Berkley and Jac had been friends for a few years, and the banter between them occurred on a regular basis. When Berkley decided to include wedding packages as a way to increase business for the resort, she'd hired Jac to be the on-site photographer.

Jac was a shifter, but she was also considered a hybrid because her cat was part ocelot, part jaguar. When she transformed, her animal was only a few sizes larger than a house cat.

I turned to Hannah with a grin. "You'll have to excuse my friends. Nobody famous ever stays here." I winked and placed my hand on the small of Hannah's back, then aimed her toward an empty seat near the end of the table. "The most excitement they get is from dealing with poachers."

"Or the occasional kidnapper," Mandy added.

She rarely talked about the time she'd been abducted by Desmond Bishop, the previous owner of the Hanford Regency. The male made the mistake of taking her when Nick and his siblings refused to sign the deed of the resort over to him. Luckily, Mandy hadn't been harmed, but the same couldn't be said for the males who worked for Bishop.

"Kidnapping, seriously?" Though Hannah's green eyes sparkled with interest, she glanced skeptically at the other females.

"Yep, so if you ever need some good information for one of your books…" Mandy said, clasping her hands together.

"I'll keep it in mind," Hannah said, setting her glasses on the table and taking a seat.

I didn't want to hover, so I leaned against the center island. "Now that you've met Berkley, Jac, and Mandy"—I pointed at each of them in turn—"would you mind explaining why you're wearing a disguise?"

"Oh, you mean this." She pulled the wig from her head and fluffed her curls. "I had it on when I arrived and thought it would be less confusing when I spoke to the person working at the reservation desk."

"Do you have problems being stalked by fans?" Berkley straightened in her seat, her tone switching to concerned business owner.

"No, not usually." Hannah placed the wig on the table, then smoothed the strands. "I know it might sound strange, but changing my appearance and pretending to be the heroine in my book helps me work through some tough scenes."

"Actually, that sounds rather smart," Jac said.

Mandy bobbed her head. "Not to mention fun."

I was afraid my friends were going to insist that Hannah let them help with one of her current scenes and was glad when Reese sauntered back into the room a few seconds later.

"Problems?" Berkley asked.

Reese shook his head. "No, I think I convinced Evan that the reports of a tiger were probably a prank, so I don't think he'll insist on checking our property for the time being."

Reese had been so focused on answering his sister that he hadn't noticed Hannah until he got closer to the table. "Oh," he said after catching a whiff of her scent and realizing she was the tiger in question.

"Hannah, this is my mate, Reese," Jac said. "He's also Berkley's brother and part owner of the resort."

"It's nice to meet you, and I'm sorry my being here has caused you so much trouble. It's just that I'd heard so many good things about your resort, and my cabin is wonderful. I thought for sure staying here would help with my writing."

Hannah was rambling and looked like she was going to have another panic attack. I hadn't gotten a chance to call my friend in Hanford about her allergy issues. But when I did, I planned to ask him if the breathing problem could also affect her in other ways, even possibly be at the root of her constricting anxiety.

"Well, it's nothing we can't handle, so don't worry about it." Berkley reached across the table and patted Hannah's hand.

"I'm sure it's not, but I think I should leave in the morning anyway," Hannah said, her smile strained.

Worrying that she posed a threat to the other guests had to be Hannah's motivation for insisting she go. One of the resort's selling points, for shifters, anyway, was being able to let their animals run in a secluded area where they didn't have to worry about being seen by any humans. It had to be one of the reasons she'd booked her stay to begin with. "No one is saying you have to leave." I pulled out the chair next to her and took a seat.

"Mitch is right. We'll figure something out," Berkley said.

"Reese will make sure you don't have to worry about the rangers swarming the property and trying to hunt you down, won't you?" Jac glared at her mate.

I'd always found the interaction between Jac and Reese

to be quite entertaining. Reese could be one of the most intimidating males I'd ever met. He was even scarier as his wolf. Yet one pursed-lip glare from Jac had the male cringing. "Of course."

I hardly knew Hannah, but the thought of her leaving and never seeing her again had my stomach clenching into a tight knot. "Why don't you stay at my place?" The words were out before I'd had a chance to consider what I was saying.

It wasn't one of my better ideas, but it was the only one I could come up with. I knew she was destined to have a mate, one she obviously hadn't met yet; otherwise, he'd be with her now. That alone should have been reason enough not to get involved. I could even try to justify my decision by telling myself that all I wanted to do was help, but it would be a lie. I'd been drawn to Hannah from the moment those beautiful green eyes had locked with mine.

"I don't want to be an imposition, and I certainly don't want to cause any problems with your girlfriend," Hannah said.

"You wouldn't be." She'd been in my home, knew I didn't live with a female, so I wasn't sure if her interest in my relationship status was purely out of politeness or if she was truly interested.

Either way, I was more than happy to provide the information. "I'm single, live alone, no girlfriends." I was pretty sure the groan I heard came from Reese, but I ignored him. My female friends were all grinning, so I clearly had their support. Berkley was the most perceptive of the three and was scrutinizing my interaction with Hannah the closest.

I thought about the kiss we'd shared, worried it might be the reason for her trepidation. I couldn't explain why I'd had the urge to kiss a complete stranger, especially one who sprouted claws and could have taken out my jugular with a single swipe. The fact that she hadn't swatted me off the bed made it even more confusing. "I work in town most of the time. The place is big enough for both of us, and I have a spare room that hasn't been used since Leah moved out."

"But what about your clinic?" Hannah bit her lower lip, seemingly unconvinced.

"My receptionist only comes in to work on Saturday mornings. The rest of the week, the place is quiet, and you'd be able to do as much writing as you want without anyone bothering you."

Now that I'd made the suggestion, I was determined to get her to agree. "I also own a few acres, so if you need to go for a run, no one will see you. I'd even be willing to go with you to make sure your cat doesn't wander off. That is, if she's forgiven me for shooting her."

"My cat actually likes…" Hannah blushed and quickly changed the subject. "Are you sure about this?"

"Absolutely, I…"

"Wait a minute." Jac held up her hand. "Did you say you shot her?" It seemed I'd been right about Berkley not telling Mandy and Jac the entire story. They were both scowling at me, only Jac looked as if she wouldn't have a problem leaving a few claw marks on my body.

When Hannah's growl drew everyone's attention, she quickly tried to cover up the protective act by clearing her throat. "It was only a dart, and if Mitch hadn't shot me, the problem with the rangers might have been a lot worse." She returned her attention to me. "It looks like you have a new houseguest."

***

HANNAH

Having done plenty of research on murder methods and serial killers before writing ten mystery novels, I was confident I'd be safe staying with Mitch. His friends seemed to think very highly of him, and I had a feeling if

I'd told him no, they would have gone out of their way to convince me to reconsider his offer.

I'd hated giving up my cabin, but was glad I wouldn't have to leave the mountain wilderness and return to my home in the city earlier then I'd planned. Berkley had even insisted on holding the cabin for me free of charge in case I changed my mind or if things didn't work out with Mitch.

My cat might be a tiger and a predator when she needed to be, but she had a laid-back personality. It had surprised me that she was enthusiastically onboard with spending the rest of our working vacation at Mitch's place.

On the return trip to his house, he drove his truck, and I'd followed him with my rental car. As soon as we arrived, he insisted on carrying my luggage inside. Rather than argue that I was capable of doing it myself, I grabbed my shoulder bag and computer case and waited in the reception area of the clinic for him to make the two trips necessary to get the four large suitcases inside.

"Are you sure you didn't leave any clothes at home?" he teased as he dragged the last case down the hallway and set it near the foot of the bed.

His spare room was smaller than the room I'd woken up in, but the queen-size bed looked comfortable, and through the open blinds on the window, I had a great view of the forest area behind his house.

"If you think this is bad, you should travel with my mother. She packs one case for each day of her trip and won't stay anywhere unless it has a five-star rating." The female also enjoyed being pampered and would never stay anywhere this close to nature. She refused to run on anything except manicured grass.

"I'll consider myself lucky, then." Mitch laughed and held out his hand. "Come on, I'll show you the rest of the house before you settle in." He took me back into the hallway and toward the part of his home I hadn't seen yet.

The corridor opened up into a nice-sized living room

complete with a fireplace surrounded with stones in varying shades of gray. I was impressed by how well-maintained and comfortable the place seemed. Most of the walls were painted an off-white. The furniture he'd selected had earth tones similar to the wood trim in each room. Even the square dinette table in the nook by the kitchen was a perfect match to the walnut stain used on the cabinets.

Two of the living room walls had pictures of mountain landscapes. He'd mentioned that his sister Leah had been living with him for a while, and I wondered if she'd influenced his choice of decor.

"Your place is really beautiful," I said.

"Thanks, I..." A loud ringing filled the air, interrupting whatever he was about to say.

Startled, I asked, "What was that?"

"Sorry, that's the buzzer for the clinic door. I know it's a little loud and annoying, but I wanted to be sure I could hear it from anywhere inside the house."

"Aren't you closed?" I asked.

"Technically, yes, but since I'm the only vet in the area, I have an open-door policy for emergencies." He turned to head toward the back of the house. "Make yourself comfortable. If you need a place to write, feel free to use the desk in my office. It's the room across the hall from your bedroom."

It seemed being around Mitch had also been good for freeing up some of my creative issues. Even though most of the daydreaming I'd done on the drive from the lodge had been about him and the kiss we'd shared earlier, I'd also come up with an idea I was certain would fix a scene I'd been struggling with.

With that in mind, I headed back to my room to grab my laptop, but instead of going into his office, I decided to use the nook in the kitchen so I could enjoy the scenic view outside.

It hadn't taken me long to get so engrossed in what I

was typing that I almost didn't hear the light footsteps approaching. At first, I thought I'd imagine the noise, until I felt small arms wrap around my leg. I leaned to the side and peeked under the table and found a young boy with the biggest chocolate-brown eyes I'd ever seen. The faint scent of bear clung to his skin. I estimated his age to be somewhere between two and three years old.

"Hey there, little one, where did you come from?" Instead of answering my question, he curled his lips into the cutest smile, then made a clawing motion and roared.

"Okay, then." I took his hand and urged him out from underneath the table.

A rush of footsteps preceded the panicked female who emerged from the hallway. Her flushed and rounded cheeks were similar to the child's. "There you are."

"I'm so sorry." She held out her arms and scooped up the child as soon as he reached for her. "He's at that curious age where all I have to do is blink and he's gone."

"It's no problem," I said.

"Trina," Mitch called from the hallway. "Did you find him?"

"We're back here," Trina answered.

Mitch showed up a few minutes later with a girl who looked to be about eight years old following behind him. Dirt smudged her nose, and some of her light brown hair had pulled loose from the braids dangling on either side of her head.

"Trina." He smiled, his gaze going from the female to me. "I see you've met Hannah." He pointed to the child beside him. "And this is Callie."

I tipped my head toward the bandage wrapped around the girl's hand and wrist. "That looks like it might hurt a little."

"Mitch says it's not bad. I've had worse." She twisted it back and forth, eliciting a frown from Trina.

I pressed my lips together to hide my amusement at her nonchalant way of dismissing the injury that no doubt worried her mother.

Trina shifted her son so he was perched on her right hip. "Callie just learned to shift and hasn't mastered climbing trees yet."

"Mom." Callie drew out the word and shot an embarrassed glare at her parent.

I crossed my arms. "You know, I can remember falling out of trees a time or two when I first learned how to shift myself."

"Really?" Her voice was edged with disbelief, a notorious trait for children her age.

"Uh-huh, but if you keep practicing, I'm sure you'll be a pro in no time."

Callie sniffed the air. "I've never met a tiger before. Are you the one the ranger who stopped by our house was looking for?"

"Callie." Trina gritted her teeth.

"What?" Callie snarled.

"It's okay." I appreciated the child's honesty and didn't want to lie to her. "Yes, that would be me."

Callie jutted out her chin. "Don't you know that you're not supposed to let humans know about us?" She shot Mitch an approving smile. "Except for Mitch, because he's our friend and always helps us."

It was hard not to grin after being scolded by a child. "That's why he's keeping a close eye on me and making sure I don't get into any more trouble."

Callie wrinkled her nose. "Eww, don't you hate having a babysitter?"

"I do." I leaned forward so I was eye level with Callie, then glanced at Mitch over my shoulder. "But he is kind of cute, so maybe it won't be so bad."

Callie giggled.

"Okay, then." Trina reached down and took her daughter's hand. "We should probably get going and let you two get back to whatever it was you were doing."

It didn't take us long to walk Trina and her children

out, then return to the kitchen.

"Now that Callie has officially dubbed you my babysitter, do you still think having me around is a good idea?" I asked.

He propped his elbows on the edge of the kitchen island. "Yep, but just because you think I'm cute doesn't mean I'm going to let you get away with anything."

I slid my hands to my hips. "Don't let it go to your head. I only said it to impress Callie."

"So you're saying you don't think I'm cute?" He slumped his shoulders and produced an exaggerated pout.

"Maybe." I flashed him a wicked grin, then headed back to the nook and my laptop.

CHAPTER FOUR

MITCH

"Mitch, did you hear what I said?" Ivy, my receptionist, waved her hand in front of my face, snapping me out of my latest daydream about Hannah.

"Sorry," I said, placing the file for my last patient in the basket on her desk. It was going to be a long day if I was already on my fourth apology for the morning.

"Is everything okay?" She tucked the blonde strand that had escaped from her ponytail behind her ear. "You seem a little distracted."

"I'm fine," I said, even though I knew I wasn't. I couldn't remember the last time I'd been so preoccupied that focusing on work was a problem. Lately, all I did was think about Hannah.

She'd only been staying at my house a few days, but I thoroughly enjoyed spending time with her. Other than her little problem with getting distracted easily, the female was witty, intelligent, and fun to be around.

Surprisingly, she had a wicked sense of humor, which made flirting with her easy. Unfortunately, and because I didn't want to do anything to make her change her mind about staying, I also had to be a perfect gentleman.

With each passing day, it was getting harder to resist the attraction I felt for her. Nights were the worst. It was difficult to get any sleep when the house was filled with her enticing scent, the desire to have her share my bed even stronger.

Worse, and even more troubling, was knowing she'd be leaving in another week, that there was a good chance I'd never see her again. Thinking about pursuing a relationship with her was futile. She would eventually find her destined mate and forget all about me.

The door going to the sidewalk outside and the main street in Ashbury opened. I'd expected to see someone wrestling with a pet carrier or tugging their animal with a lead, not my sister struggling to get inside.

I scowled and hurried around the counter to hold the door for her. "Leah, aren't you under doctor's orders to stay at home in bed with your feet up?" I was very protective when it came to my younger sister. Even more so now that I was going to be an uncle.

I leaned forward and gave her a semi-hug, doing my best not to push against her protruding belly, proof that she was a week or so away from delivering her first child.

She frowned. "No, they were Bryson's orders, not the doctors."

I was in complete agreement with her mate. The thought of her driving down the mountain alone was worrisome. If I hadn't made her a promise long ago not to be an interfering and overbearing brother, I would have shared my concerns.

"Seriously, if it was up to him, I'd never get any exercise." She patted my cheek. "Besides, his mother assures me that walking is the best thing now that I'm so close."

As far as in-laws went, Leah had done well. Glenda Cruise might have strong opinions on pretty much everything, but she was likable and constantly mothered my sister. "Well, if Glenda says it's okay, then it must be." My chuckle earned me a smack on the arm.

"So, what brings you into town? More shopping for the baby?" Between Bryson's relatives, our extended family at the lodge, and me, my new niece or nephew wasn't going to need anything for quite a while.

"Berkley needed to come into town for supplies and thought Hannah might enjoy getting out of the house."

My pulse raced at the mention of Hannah's name, but I did my best to appear uninterested. I was more concerned about the time my sister was spending with my new houseguest. Unlike my mother, who was constantly after me to settle down, Leah was good about not meddling in my personal life.

It wouldn't, however, stop her from trying to find out why I'd invited a female I didn't know to stay in my home. Since I hadn't offered an explanation, it appeared she'd gone straight to the source.

Berkley, on the other hand, already knew why Hannah was staying with me, so I had no idea why she'd suggested they take a road trip. I had a feeling she was up to something, but didn't get a chance to question my sister about my suspicions. The door opened again, and the sound of laughter filtered into the room. Hannah walked inside, her smile beaming, her strawberry-blonde curls loosely draped over her shoulders.

The day before, I'd arrived at home to find Hannah wearing a shiny black wig with straight strands that reached the middle of her back. She had quite a selection of wigs in her disguise collection, and although all of them complemented her appearance, I preferred her real hair.

"Hey, guys." Berkley waved at Ivy as she walked inside.

"Hi, Berkley. Who's your friend?" Ivy asked.

"This is Hannah," Berkley said as she closed the door behind her. "She's visiting for a couple of weeks."

Feeding the rumor mill was a favorite pastime for many of the local residents. Ivy was a great employee, but if extracting information was classified by levels, she would rank as an expert.

I stepped between my visitors and my inquisitive employee, then changed the subject before someone slipped and told her Hannah was staying at my place and not the lodge. "Not that I don't enjoy seeing you, Leah, but did you have a reason for stopping by?"

"Yes, we were going to take Hannah down to Driscoll's Diner and thought you might like to join us for lunch." Leah rubbed her belly. "And I'm hoping we go soon, because this little guy is starving."

I raised a brow. "The baby is talking to you now?"

Leah huffed. "No, but I'm starving."

Berkley laughed and draped an arm across my sister's shoulder. "You've been saying that since you first found out you were pregnant."

"Yeah, well, it's true." Leah winked at Ivy, who was doing a terrible job pretending she was staring at her computer screen and not listening to our conversation.

"Sounds like an emergency to me." Hannah glanced at me, then tilted her head toward the door.

I wasn't about to refuse the lunch request. "It does, doesn't it?" I slipped off my lab coat and hung it on one of the hooks mounted on a nearby wall. "Ivy, do you want me to bring you back anything?" She had a dentist appointment later in the day and had already asked if she could work through her lunch so she could leave early.

"No, I'm good. My roommate made spaghetti last night, so I brought my lunch," she said.

I held the door open and waited for the females to exit. "I should be back in about an hour. Call my cell if you have any problems," I said, even though I was hoping nothing came up that would keep me from spending a little more time with Hannah.

The weather was pleasant, with only a few clouds sprinkled across the blue sky. Since Driscoll's was only a few blocks away, Leah insisted we walk. The place was normally busy during the lunch hour, but even going at my sister's slow pace, we arrived ahead of the crowd.

"We'd like one of the big booths in the back," Leah told the waitress, who greeted us with a handful of menus as soon as we walked through the door.

"I don't think you'll fit. Are you sure you wouldn't rather sit at a table?" The up-and-down glance I gave Leah earned me a sidelong glare and another smack on the arm.

As soon as Leah slid across the orange faux-leather seat so she could sit by the window, Berkley quickly squeezed into the spot next to her, making sure Hannah ended up sitting next to me. I couldn't prove it, but I'd swear the maneuver had been preplanned.

Leah glanced down at the two-inch gap between her belly and the edge of the table, then smirked. "See? There's plenty of room."

"Yeah, but if you expand while you eat, I might have to go get the crowbar out of my truck." I grinned.

"Are they always like this?" Hannah asked Berkley.

Berkley shrugged, then went back to perusing her menu. "Pretty much, but you get used to it."

The booth we'd been given was positioned along the far wall of the building and gave us a panoramic view of the entire diner. So far, the seats on either side of ours were empty. After a few minutes, Leah laid her menu on the table and leaned forward as much as she was able to see around Berkley, no doubt looking for someone to take our order.

"Mitch, isn't that Avery?" Leah asked.

I followed the direction of her gaze and stifled a groan when I saw the female she'd mentioned sauntering toward us. Avery was a wolf shifter who happened to work at the diner. I'd met her shortly after moving to Ashbury. She hadn't been happy that I'd politely turned down her numerous invitations to show me around the area. Though from her flirtatious insinuations, I was fairly certain showing me the sights wasn't what she was interested in.

Every time I visited the diner while she was working, she did everything possible to see if she could change my mind. Telling her no hadn't seem to matter, so I'd quickly learned her schedule and avoided coming into the restaurant when I knew she'd be there.

"Isn't she the one who…"

I cut off the rest of what my sister was about to say by nudging her leg with the side of my knee. Leah was well aware of the situation. She'd been having lunch with me the last time Avery had made one of her offers. The last thing I needed was for her to inadvertently say something about the other female in front of Hannah.

Ashbury was a small community, and running into someone I'd dated was bound to happen, but I would have preferred it be anyone other than Avery.

Of the occasional dates I'd been on, none of them had turned into something steady or anything long-lasting.

When Leah or my mother pestered me about my lack of a relationship, I'd used being a sole proprietor with a business that required unusual hours as my excuse. There were plenty of women who lived in Ashbury and the surrounding area, but none of them held my interest longer than a few weeks, let alone a few months. A fact that worried my mother and earned me more than a little teasing from my sister.

It was too late to suggest going somewhere else to eat. The closer Avery got, the more I wanted to kick myself for agreeing to have lunch at Driscoll's. If I hadn't been so excited about spending time with Hannah, I wouldn't have forgotten there was a good chance Avery would be working.

She arrived at our table wearing a dress-type peach uniform and carrying a tray containing four glasses filled with ice water. "Mitch, it's been a while," she said as she set a glass in front of each of us. She stood with her hip inches away from my arm, twirling the end of her long braid. "Did you stop by to tell me you changed your mind about my offer?"

Hannah gripped her menu so tight, I could hear the plastic crinkle. "Offer?" She glared at Avery, and her voice deepened, edged with an animalistic quality. The green in her eyes was a lot darker than it had been a few minutes ago.

I'd been around shifters enough to realize Hannah's reaction stemmed from being protective, a behavior that warmed me to the core.

"When Mitch first arrived in Ashbury, I told him I'd be more than happy to show him some of the sights the tourists don't know about," Avery said, her tone smug.

"I'll bet you did," Berkley muttered, then rolled her eyes.

I got the impression there was a history between the two females that I didn't know anything about, and hoped that whatever it was didn't escalate past the two of them sneering at each other.

Shifters had different rules about the way they handled things, and thanks to Reese, Berkley knew how to fight. I had no doubt that even in her human form, she'd have no problem taking care of Avery.

Avery ignored Berkley's remark. "I'm sure there's still one or two more places you haven't seen yet, so if you change your mind, you know how to reach me." She sneered and held Hannah's gaze as she brushed her fingertips along my sleeve.

I wasn't sure if Avery was taunting Hannah out of stupidity or spite. Either way, I wasn't going to let it continue. "As I said before, I appreciate your generosity, but I'm not interested." I scooted away from her touch, then leaned back in my seat and draped my arm across the booth behind Hannah.

Avery pursed her lips. If she'd been in her wolf form, I imagined her animal's fur would be bristling.

"I don't mean to be rude, but if you're done flirting with my brother, would you mind taking our order?" Leah grinned at Hannah, then waved her menu at Avery until she took it.

It seemed Hannah had gained a friend in my sister.

Avery glanced at the watch on her wrist. "Oh, darn. It looks like it's time for my break." She glanced at the waitress who'd just seated a family of four in the booth to our right. "Madison, can you be a sweetheart and take this table's order?" Avery's question sounded more like a threat and had the younger female cringing.

"Oh, uh, sure," Madison stammered.

As soon as Madison reached into her pocket and pulled out an order pad and pen, Avery dismissed us without saying another word.

Berkley kept her eyes trained on Avery until she disappeared through a set of swinging doors at the back of the diner. "Huh, that's strange."

"What's strange?" I had a bad feeling I wasn't going to like the answer, but decided to ask anyway.

Berkley gave the doors one last glance before reaching for her glass of water. "Avery doesn't usually give up that easily."

***

HANNAH

I might not be able to scent well, but I didn't have any problem recognizing a shifter or determining their animal. And it certainly didn't take me long to figure out that Avery was a wolf who enjoyed stalking and using males. She was a predator of the worst kind. She liked to lure males into her bed, then toss them away when she was finished with them.

The diner's unflattering peach uniform didn't disguise Avery's beauty. With her shiny black hair and dark eyes lined with long lashes, it was easy to see why males would be attracted to her.

I admired Mitch for having enough sense to see past her appearance to the unpleasant side of her personality and avoid going out with her. What I didn't appreciate was Avery's persistence.

When she'd dared to put her fingers on Mitch, my cat had come close to forcing a shift. I wasn't sure what was going on with my animal. She was acting as if Mitch was her mate, and it had taken every ounce of restraint I'd possessed to keep her from shredding some fur off the mangy wolf's backside.

The only thing that seemed to calm her was having Mitch lean a little closer and drape his arm across the booth behind me. I deduced from Berkley's condescending remark that she knew Avery well and didn't care for the female either. It didn't seem to matter that I'd known her and Leah for only a couple of days. They'd given me their support and friendship unconditionally, and for that I was extremely grateful.

Once Avery disappeared and Madison had taken over as our waitress, the lunch I had with Mitch, Berkley, and Leah had been quite enjoyable. Brother and sister continued their playful banter, with Berkley and me occasionally joining the conversation.

After Berkley's comment about Avery not giving up, I'd been mildly concerned that she'd make a reappearance. Madison informing us that Avery had gone home sick should have eased my lingering anxiety, but it didn't.

"Are you sure I can't get you anything else?" Madison asked as she removed the last empty plate from the table.

"I think we're good," Mitch said.

No sooner had Madison walked away from the table than a muted melody came from the purse sitting on the seat between Leah and Berkley. Leah slipped her hand inside, pulled out her cell phone, and scowled at the screen. "I'm surprised he didn't call sooner."

Berkley leaned closer to get a glimpse of the phone, then silently mouthed Bryson's name.

"Hey, honey, how's your day going?" Leah's voice oozed all kinds of sweetness when she answered the call. She listened for a few seconds, then said, "You know these hormones make me forgetful. I was sure I told you I was going shopping with Berkley."

"Uh-huh." Leah rolled her eyes, so I could only imagine what her mate was saying. "We decided to have lunch with Mitch. You do know if anything happens to me that my brother… Yes, I know he's a vet, but…" Leah pressed her lips together.

On the drive into Ashbury, Berkley had mentioned that Leah's mate was extremely overprotective and lived up to his reputation of being a grumpy bear. She'd told me the male hadn't been much of a conversationalist before he'd met Mitch's sister, but based on what I could hear of the conversation he was having with Leah, it appeared he had plenty to say to her now.

"Fine, we're leaving." Leah tossed the phone into her purse. "Apparently, according to my mate"—Leah made quotes with her fingers—"if I don't get my backside home immediately, he's going to scour the town until he finds me."

Berkley giggled. "You know he's going to be worse after the baby comes, don't you?"

Leah smirked. "Not if he ever wants to have sex again."

"Geez, Leah, we're eating." Mitch groaned as he glanced at the surrounding booths, no doubt checking to see how many people had overheard his sister.

"Technically, were finished." I smiled at Leah.

"Don't encourage her." He grinned as he scolded me, then snatched the check for our meals out of Berkley's hand and scooted out of the booth.

"Hey," she snarled. "We invited you to lunch, remember?"

"You can pay next time." He motioned for her to get out of the booth, then held out his hand to help Leah to her feet. "Come on, let's get you on your way before

Bryson decides to come looking for you."

He waited for Berkley and Leah to go ahead of us, then walked beside me with his hand placed on the small of my back. His gentle touch made my cat purr. She wanted to rub all over him, and I was tempted to let her. Compromising, I leaned a little closer, my shoulder brushing his. "Thank you for lunch."

"Thank you for asking." We'd reached the cashier, so Mitch pulled his wallet out of his pocket.

Madison had done a great job, and I wanted to personally give her a tip. I waited for her to finish taking another order. "Give me a second, I'll be right back," I said to Mitch, then hurried to catch her before she reached the food counter.

"This is for you." I placed a twenty-dollar bill in her hand.

Madison stared at the money, then back at me, her cheeks flushing red. "This is way too much."

I curled my hand over hers when she tried to give it back. "Consider it hazard pay for having to work with Avery."

"Thanks." She grinned and quickly tucked the money into the pocket of her apron.

The group had been waiting for me outside, so as soon as I joined them, we headed back to Mitch's clinic.

We were halfway there when Berkley stopped and glanced behind us. "Is it my imagination, or are we being followed?"

It was a good thing Berkley's wolf had been paying attention, because my cat had been too busy focusing on Mitch to notice any possible danger.

On the drive into town, Berkley had shared some stories about the summers she'd stayed with her grandfather. She'd spent a lot of time hanging out with Mandy and getting to know a few of the locals.

We'd been moving at a slower pace so Leah wouldn't have to rush. We slowed even further so we could see who

Berkley was talking about. I wasn't sure if Mitch stepping in front of me to block my view had been an accident or if he was intentionally trying to protect me.

"You mean the person with the newspaper, the one who just walked into that light pole?" Leah asked.

By the time I peeked around Mitch, all I caught was a glimpse of the person's navy-blue hooded jacket before they ducked inside the ice-cream shop.

"Is it anyone you know?" Mitch asked me, his voice laced with concern.

I shook my head. "I'm afraid I didn't get much of a look."

"Maybe we should go check it out." Leah made it only a few steps before Mitch placed a hand on his sister's elbow. "The clinic's this way." He aimed her in the direction we were originally headed.

"Do you think one of your fans found out you were here?" Berkley asked as she moved to walk on Leah's other side.

"I didn't even share my travel plans with my parents, so I don't think anyone knows where I am. Except, of course, for you guys." I hadn't been stalked in a long time and had taken a few precautions to make sure I wasn't followed.

My best friend, Sydney, was the only one who knew where I'd gone. I didn't mention that she was a tour guide, was currently working on a job with bad cell reception, and wouldn't get the message I'd left her until she returned home at the end of the week.

It was too bad Sydney hadn't been available to travel with me. She would have loved staying in the cabin at the resort and checking out the area. Once I was finished with my book, I might take a real vacation and bring her back here with me. But seeing Mitch again and knowing we could never have a real relationship, not because he was human, but because I still held out hope that I would eventually find my mate, immediately put an end to the idea.

"Why not?" Leah asked. "Won't they be worried about you?"

I didn't want to explain the dynamics of my family, but I didn't want my new friends to be concerned either. "My father, possibly, but my mother would have turned it into a vacation with a daily itinerary planning out every minute of my day." I sighed. "I never would have gotten any writing done if she'd come with me."

I glanced over my shoulder one last time before we crossed the street to reach the clinic and didn't see anyone who looked as if they might be following us. I hoped I'd been correct in my assumption that the person Berkley had seen wasn't an overzealous fan or a possible stalker. I certainly didn't want them following my friends home or finding out where Mitch lived.

"You know, Hannah, I only have one appointment scheduled for this afternoon," Mitch said. "I'm sure I can get my assistant to cover for me. If you don't mind waiting a few minutes, I'd be happy to give you a ride back to my place." He leaned closer and lowered his voice so no one other than Berkley and Leah could hear him. "Maybe we'd even have time to take your cat for a run. That is if you're up for it."

"I'd love to…" I blurted a little too eagerly. With my cat's unusual behavior and the feelings I was developing for Mitch, I should have said no and ridden back with Berkley and Leah. I also should have refused their invitation to take a trip into town. It was hard to tell Berkley no when she'd insisted, then taunted me with inviting Mitch to lunch.

My cat, the unruly animal, perked at the idea of spending more time alone with Mitch. I had to swallow to keep her approving growl from slipping into my voice. "I mean, are you sure you don't mind?"

"Not at all." He grinned, then moved out of reach before adding, "I'll even leave my dart gun at home."

CHAPTER FIVE

It was nearing four in the afternoon by the time Mitch and I arrived at his home. His appointment had taken a little longer than he'd expected, which turned out to be a good thing as far as catching up on my writing. Since I never went anywhere without my portable tablet, I spent the additional time sitting in his office and working on my manuscript. It seems my run-in with Avery had an inspiring effect that enabled me to draft an entire scene in no time.

Mitch unlocked the door leading into his home clinic, then held it open for me to enter. "We should have a couple more hours of sunlight, if you're interested in going for a short run?"

I understood his concern. I could see in the dark, so walking through the forest at night wouldn't present the same problem for me as it did for him. "My cat and I are definitely interested." I received an approving chuff from my animal as I followed him down the hall. She'd been cooped up since our misadventure had gotten us into trouble and badly needed to get out.

I desperately wanted to burn off the anxiety I'd been experiencing since the unpleasant encounter with Avery. It was a good thing the female wasn't around, because restraining my cat would be impossible. I also hoped that getting some fresh air might help me sort out the issue of my animal's fixation with Mitch. Something that wasn't going to end well for either of us.

"Great, then I'll go change and meet you out back."

Mitch had seen me in my animal form, but this was going to be the first time I shifted while we were both awake. I stood in the middle of my bedroom, taking longer than necessary to contemplate the best way to handle transitioning from a naked human into my cat in front of him. Embarrassment was not the problem. I'd shifted plenty of times around other males who were friends or members of my family.

Mitch was human, raised in a different world, and I wasn't sure if walking around his house naked was an acceptable thing to do. After coming up with what I hoped would be a suitable compromise, I stripped, then grabbed the blanket draped along the foot of the bed, and secured it around my chest.

When I stepped out onto the deck, Mitch was leaning against the railing, staring at the surrounding forest. He'd changed into an old pair of worn jeans, a T-shirt, and hiking boots. The outfit suited him, giving him a rugged look and making him even more appealing.

He smiled, his gaze slowly roaming over me as if he was hoping I'd lose my grip on the blanket. "Is your tiger shy?" he teased as he reached for the backpack sitting near his feet before tugging the strap over one shoulder.

"No, and neither am I." I ignored the heat rising on my cheeks that seemed to say otherwise. "Would you mind putting these in your bag?" I handed Mitch the pair of sweats, shirt, and walking shoes I'd grabbed before leaving my room.

"Not at all, but do you really need them?" he asked.

"One-sided conversations are a little boring, so I thought I'd shift and visit with you on the way back."

"I like that plan." He stepped off the deck, giving me plenty of room to maneuver.

I sensed his nervousness and could tell he was a little worried about how my cat was going to respond to him. I wanted to reassure him that she didn't hold a grudge over the shooting incident, but figured it would be easier to show him.

I dropped the towel, catching an admiring gaze from Mitch before letting my animal take over.

I jumped from the deck, my paws touching the ground a few feet away from him. My cat was larger than a regular tiger, and I had to give him credit for not backing away.

"Uh, Hannah," Mitch said when my cat started purring, then rubbed the side of her body along his legs as if she wanted to mark him from top to bottom. "I'd expected some sniffing, maybe a little growling…"

Being attracted to a male was a normal byproduct of being part human. It was completely different from recognizing the male I was meant to bond with, and I was confused even more by my cat's current behavior. On the few occasions I'd gone on a run with a male I'd been interested in, my cat usually acted indifferent, sometimes even bored. She'd never responded this possessively toward any of them.

I wasn't a complete novice when it came to relationships. I'd had a few, but I'd never let any of them get serious, because, like most shifters, I wanted to find my true mate. I'd also accepted the fact that having bad allergies, coupled with the problems it caused my cat when it came to scenting things, pretty much ensured finding the male was never going to happen, not unless he happened to find me first.

"Does this mean I'm forgiven for shooting her?" He chuckled, bracing his legs to keep from being knocked to the ground.

I placed my head under his hand to show him there were no hard feelings, then encouraged him to run his hand through my fur. He took his time smoothing his hand along my thick coat, stopping occasionally to knead my back.

My cat purred even louder and would have gladly rolled on her back and let him run his hand along her stomach. Once my cat was satisfied that Mitch was covered with her scent, that no other female would dare mess with him, I took the lead and headed into the forest.

I burst into a run, letting the freedom temper the tension rippling through my body. After a few minutes, I stopped and waited for Mitch to catch up, then matched my pace to his.

I stopped to smell an occasional patch of wildflowers. My allergies had kicked in the minute I'd stepped into the forest so no matter how much I sniffed I couldn't get a whiff of their floral fragrance.

Every now and then, I caught sight of a butterfly, but before I could chase after it, Mitch tugged on the end of my tail to keep me on track.

The third time he grabbed my tail for no reason, I head-butted his leg. "Hey," he groaned. "I'm supposed to be keeping you out of trouble, remember?"

I responded with a chuff and nudged his leg, then quickly jumped out of his way when he reached for my tail again.

Before long, we'd reached a stream, and I couldn't resist romping and splashing through the water. I also couldn't resist shaking off the excess moisture and catching him with the spray when I was done.

With a huff, he wiped the wet sprinkles off his face. "I want you to know I will be getting even with you later." He took a seat on the trunk of an old tree that looked as if it had been uprooted years ago.

When he unzipped his backpack and pulled out a bottle of water, I pawed the bag, hoping he'd understand that I wanted my clothes. "Are you trying to tell me you'd like to change back now?"

I bobbed my head and sat back on my haunches, waiting for him to set my clothes and shoes on the log next to him.

"Let me know if you need any help," he said, grabbing his bag as he got up and walked a few feet away before giving me his back.

I quickly shifted into my human form so I could respond to his taunt. "I think I can handle it, but thanks."

Mitch glanced at the sky through a gap in the trees. "We should start heading back. I'd rather not get stuck out here in the dark."

What was left of the sunlight was fading, the sparse clouds tinted with pinks and yellows. "Oh, I don't know, it might be kind of fun watching you walk into trees."

"Shifter humor…so not funny," he said with a snort, then took my hand. "Come on, I know a shortcut."

His so-called shortcut took us through an area that didn't have any worn trails, wasn't exactly level, and hadn't seen much hiking. It did, however, lead us back to an area I recognized that wasn't far from his house.

Snapping twigs echoed in the distance too far away and faint for Mitch to hear. Without drawing his attention, I casually glanced around the area, searching for the source of the noise. I didn't see anything out of the ordinary or notice any small creatures scurrying under bushes. "Do you ever get any bears or wolves out here?"

"Seriously?" He shot a disbelieving glance in my direction.

"I was talking about the real ones, not your friends."

"Not usually this close to the house. Why?" he asked.

"I could have sworn I heard something."

Concerned, he stopped to glance around. "Noises carry in the woods. Is it possible you heard a rabbit or a squirrel?"

"Probably." My ability to smell might not function well,

but my enhanced hearing worked fine. I was certain the steps had been made by something a lot heavier.

"If it makes you feel any better, I have motion-activated lights on the front and back of the house. If anything gets close, we'll know about it." He tucked a curl behind my ear. "I won't let anything happen to you."

His willingness to protect me warmed me to the core. I refrained from telling him it wasn't me I was worried about, but him. I could take care of myself. At least most of the time.

When we started walking again, I remained on alert, determined to keep Mitch safe and make sure nothing trailed us back to his home.

CHAPTER SIX

MITCH

No female had ever affected me the way Hannah did. The more I was around her, the harder it got to be away from her. The uneasiness I'd been experiencing since the ordeal with Avery at the restaurant hadn't subsided, especially after Berkley pointed out the person she thought was following us.

It only got worse after Hannah mentioned hearing something in the woods during our hike. I got the impression from the way she'd tensed that it was more than a small creature bounding about in the woods.

I'd been reluctant to leave her at home alone and had almost closed the clinic for the day. I didn't care that she was part tiger or better equipped than I was to deal with an intruder. I was concerned about her welfare and had called several times to check on her.

As it was, I'd taken off early and left Noah Ross, the vet who worked part-time for me, alone to cover appointments. He'd started working for me a year ago while he'd finished his training, then stayed on after he'd acquired his license.

Since he lived in Hanover, he split his time between a clinic there and working a couple of days a week for me. I didn't have a problem leaving him by himself. Besides being great with the patients and their owners, he was capable of handling any walk-ins or emergencies he encountered.

Normally, the drive home from Ashbury was enjoyable. Taking in the scenic mountain backdrop of spruce and pine trees intermingled with the occasional ash was usually relaxing after a long day on my feet. Today, the overwhelming need to spend time with Hannah, to make sure she was safe, made the drive seem a lot longer.

By the time I'd parked my truck and headed for the house, my anxiety had reached a higher level. It immediately tapered when I walked inside and was greeted by the smell of freshly baked cookies. The pleasing aroma brought back memories of the short time Leah had stayed with me before she'd met Bryson.

Of course, when my sister baked sweets, at least while she was staying with me, it usually meant she'd been upset about something. I hoped that wasn't the case with Hannah. She'd seemed happy about the progress she was making on her book when I'd left that morning, so I hoped the cookies weren't a sign something had changed.

Even though I'd offered her the use of my office, I'd usually find her typing away on her laptop at the table on the deck. I hadn't called to tell her I was coming home early, so I figured I'd find her outside.

I didn't want to startle her, but calling out her name would have been moot. She enjoyed listening to music while she wrote and had a wide selection programmed into her phone. Her favorites ranged from country western to rock and included a few upbeat inspirational tunes. Like all shifters, she had enhanced hearing, but with buds stuck in her ears, she wouldn't be able to hear me.

I pushed the door open and slowly peeked outside, then frowned after finding the area empty and no sign of

Hannah. If she'd been baking, she could have decided to work inside. As soon as I closed the glass door, I heard moaning coming from the opposite side of the living room. My chest tightened as I imagined all kinds of scenarios ending with her being hurt, possibly at the hands of someone who'd been stalking her. "Hannah!" I yelled as I hurried toward the kitchen.

Past the center island, I got a glimpse of a bloodied butcher knife lying on the floor next to a pair of bare feet. The pounding of my racing heart throbbed against my temples. I rushed around the corner, found Hannah lying on the floor, and struggled to get air into my lungs. Her eyes were closed, and she was dressed in a silky turquoise night gown, the hem touching the top of her thighs and barely covering her matching panties. What drew my attention most was the patch of blood on the right side of her chest and more pooling on the floor beside her head.

Before I could kneel down to check her pulse, Hannah opened her green eyes. "Hey, Mitch." She smiled and held her hand out to me. "You're back early."

With shaking hands, I helped her off the floor, trying to get my brain to reconcile what I was seeing with what she'd said. "What the…" I thought she'd been injured or, worse, killed. I couldn't believe the only topic on her mind was my early arrival. "What the hell happened?" I spit out the words a little more harshly than I'd meant to.

"Nothing." She frowned and took a step back, nearly stepping in the blood on the floor.

"Sorry." I softened my tone and reached for her hand. "When I found you on the floor, I thought… Are you sure you're all right?"

"I'm fine. Why wouldn't I be?" She took a step closer.

I raised a brow and glanced at the knife, then at the mess behind her.

Hannah widened her eyes. "Oh, that. It's not what you think. Well, it is sort of, but…" She smiled and rubbed my arm. "Remember when I told you if I get stuck on details,

I sometimes like to reenact my murder scenes?"

"Yes, but where did all the blood come from?" I hadn't seen a wound on her chest or anywhere else on her body and couldn't figure out how the puddle had gotten on the floor. She'd already told me she didn't believe in hurting smaller animals, so I was curious where it came from.

"It's fake." She grinned and swiped her finger through the patch on her skin. "I found a great recipe online." She held the coated finger in front of my face. "It looks almost like the real thing, don't you think?"

"It sure had me fooled." My accelerated pulse was slowing, and I was able to breathe normally again.

"You don't have to worry about the floor, because this stuff doesn't leave a stain." She licked her finger, then walked over to the sink. "I'll have this mess cleaned up in no time." She wrung out a dishcloth after dousing it with water.

The timer on the stove buzzed, making me jump. I quickly pressed the button to turn off the annoying noise. The light was on inside the oven, and I could see a pan filled with cookies through the glass pane.

"Would you mind pulling those out so they don't burn?" She was on her hands and knees, wiping up the fake blood. "The mitts are next to the stove."

"Is baking part of your reenactment?" I asked as I pulled out the pan and set it on the cooling rack she'd placed on the counter.

"No, those are for you." She swiped the last of the mess on the floor, then walked over and picked up the knife. "The reenactment was to help me get a better idea of how the crime scene would look so I could explain it more vividly to my readers."

Hannah was an extremely intelligent and beautiful woman, but seemed oblivious to the effect she was having on me. When she bent over, my breath hitched. Her nightgown had risen a few inches, and I got a much better view of the underwear clinging tightly to her backside. A view that had parts of my body reacting, the uncomfortable evidence pressing against the inside of my pants. I was afraid if I had to deal with any more excitement, I was going to lose consciousness from lack of air long before my heart gave out.

"I wanted to do something nice for you, and Leah told me how much you like chocolate chip cookies."

Even with a knife in one hand and a cloth soaked with fake blood in the other, she was an adorable sight. Several curls had dropped across her forehead and continued to hang in her eyes even after she puffed at them.

"Thank you." I brushed the hair from her face, tempted to taste her lips, but pressed a gentle kiss to her cheek instead.

***

HANNAH

"It's the least I could do after all you've done for me." I hadn't been able to stop thinking about that wonderful kiss Mitch had given me the first day we'd met and truly hoped he planned to do more than place a chaste kiss on my cheek. And if he did, I didn't want to be standing there with my hands full, unable to touch him. I walked over to the sink, rinsed out the dishcloth, then placed the knife in the dishwasher.

Mitch chuckled. "Yeah, I can see where shooting you in the rear would earn me cookies." He snatched one from the pan and took a bite. "Not bad," he said after swallowing, then finished the cookie off in two more bites.

"I almost forgot." He reached into his pocket and pulled out an orange bottle with a white cap resembling those used for prescriptions. "Remember me telling you about my friend Wyatt Thomas, the one who works at the lab in Hanford?"

"Yes, why?"

"He stopped by the clinic this morning and dropped these off for you." Mitch grinned and handed me the bottle. "He said you shouldn't experience any side effects, but if you do, we need to let him know so he can make some adjustments." He opened a cabinet door, retrieved a glass, and filled it half full with water. "For right now, take one a day."

I nervously removed the lid, then stared at the contents. There were enough pale yellow oval pills to last at least a month. I popped one into my mouth, then followed it with a swallow of water. "Did he mention how long it would take to see results?"

"He said it varies with species, but usually no more than twenty-four hours."

"That means by tomorrow, I could…" The ramifications of the pills actually working, the prospect of being able to scent properly and have a normal life, was overwhelming. I set the glass and the bottle on the counter, then threw myself at Mitch, catching him around the neck in a tight hug. "I don't know how to thank you." My eyes filled with moisture, my voice crackling with a sob.

"Hey." He kept one hand on my hip and wiped a tear from my cheek with the other. "No thanks are necessary. I was glad to help."

I was feeling braver than normal, and with his mouth only inches from mine, I couldn't resist going for the kiss I'd wanted him to give me earlier. His hesitation to respond lasted less than a second. Before I knew it, he'd dominated the kiss and had my cat whimpering and me moaning.

When he finally released me, we were both panting. "I know I said you didn't need to do anything to thank me, but if you want to do that again, I won't complain."

"I kissed you because I've wanted to for days, not because you're trying to help me with my allergy problem."

"For days, huh?" His hands tightened around my waist.

"I don't suppose this kissing fantasy of yours includes other things, does it?" He wiggled his brows.

I pressed my palms against his chest. "No, I think that was it," I said, not certain I was courageous enough to mention what those things were, at least not yet.

"Are you sure? Because I could…" He nuzzled my neck, nipping my earlobe, his hands slipping a little lower.

My cat purred, insisting that I finish what I'd started. Even if he wasn't my mate, there was no denying my animal and I both wanted Mitch and desired more of his touch. The next thing I knew, I'd climbed him like a tree, my legs wrapped tightly around his waist. Obviously, he'd been craving the same thing. When he gripped my backside to hold me close, he rubbed his hard erection against the part of my body that ached for his attention the most.

"What do think about continuing your reenactment in my bedroom?" He left the kitchen and headed for the hallway. "I'm sure I can come up with some stimulating ways to help with your writing."

"It might take me a while to get inspired. Are you willing to give me more than one demonstration?" I grazed his throat with my teeth.

He sucked in a breath, his steps faltering, his grip on my backside tightening. "I'll give you as many demonstrations as you want, but if you keep that up, they won't be in the bedroom."

I glanced at the plush carpet in the hallway, then nipped his neck again. "I can handle a few rug burns if you can."

He groaned, then muttered, "Killing me." After taking the first doorway, which happened to be his room, not mine, he landed us sideways in the middle of his bed.

We were lying on our sides, still facing each other, our bodies entangled the way they were when we'd entered the room. "That probably could have been a little more graceful."

"At least you made it to the bed." I laughed, pushing the hair that had fallen over his forehead back into place.

"Yes, I did," he stated proudly before his lips found mine again.

The kiss was different from the others. There was a drawn-out tenderness, as if he was committing the sampling to memory. The intense effect sent spirals of heat through my system. The moment I parted my lips, he accepted the invitation. He deepened the kiss with his tongue, his movements eager, possessive. By the time he pulled away, I was breathless and my cat was whimpering for more.

"Hannah," he panted, just as affected by the kiss as I was.

"Yes?"

He fingered the strap of my nightgown. "The next part of my presentation requires less clothing."

"Of course." I tried to sound serious. "Whatever you need." I unwrapped my leg from his hip so he could slide off the bed. While he hastened to remove his clothes, I did the same with my gown and panties, then tossed them on the floor. After repositioning myself so I lay along the length of the bed, I took the time to admire his naked body. My gaze landed on his thick, hard shaft, and the room suddenly seemed a lot warmer. "You're right. A reenactment without clothes is much more inspiring."

He noticed the direction of my gaze and grinned. "Appreciating the visual effects?"

I rolled my eyes and snorted at his arrogance. "Yes, but props only work if you know how to use them."

"Oh, I definitely know how to use them." He opened the drawer in the nightstand by the table and pulled out a condom. Once he'd seen to our protection, he started at the end of the bed, then slowly crawled toward me. Mitch might not be a shifter, but his movements reminded me of a predator. By the time he finished skimming my ankles and pushing my legs apart so he could settle his hips between my thighs, I was trembling.

"I think I'll start here." He braced on one arm and ran a finger along my throat, trailing lower along the dip between my breasts. "Please feel free at any time to let me know how I'm doing."

He took my raised brow as a signal to proceed, then lowered his head over my chest. The instant he sucked my nipple into his mouth, I gasped. He suckled and teased the nub until I was moaning and squirming.

"How am I doing so far?" He didn't give me a chance to answer before capturing my lips. When I reached for his shoulders, he took my hands and pinned them above my head. "Sorry, but this is not a hands-on demonstration."

He shifted his weight, his erection rubbing against my center and making the growing ache between my legs almost unbearable.

"You really need to get to the high point of your presentation," I growled. "Like now." I dug my heels into the back of his legs.

He chuckled, aligning his shaft with my opening. "If you insist." His thrust was hard and deep. His ability to read my body, to anticipate what I needed was uncanny. Each stroke he made was an exquisite torment that pushed me closer to pleasurable release. When he rolled his hips and adjusted to a new angle, my world exploded, and the strongest orgasm I'd ever experienced tore through me.

After several more strokes and drawing out my climax, he made a final thrust and found his own release.

He collapsed on top of me, nuzzling my neck, his warm breath making me shiver. "Now, what was that you were saying about props?" he rasped.

CHAPTER SEVEN

HANNAH

I snuggled deeper into the blankets, feeling completely sated and enjoying the last remnants of a dream that involved Mitch and wildflowers. I slid my hand along the sheet, searching for his warm body, and found his side of the bed cool and empty. After the numerous times we'd made love, then spent the rest of the night entangled in each other's arms, I'd hoped he cared enough to be around when I woke up in the morning.

I should have known better than to want or expect something more from him. From what Leah had shared with me about her brother, I'd gleaned that he liked his solitary life and avoided relationships and the complications associated with them. It shouldn't matter that I'd come to care for him a great deal over the last week. He wasn't my mate, and in a few days, my vacation would end. I'd be going home and would most likely never see him again.

I rolled onto my side, tamping down my disappointment at the upcoming loss and feeling as if I was a discarded one-night stand. Knowing I couldn't hide from him forever and needed to get out of bed, I forced my eyes open with a groan and was greeted by a beautiful handpicked bouquet of pale purple blossoms he'd left for me on his pillow.

Warmed by his thoughtfulness, I picked up one of the stems and placed the soft petals beneath my nose. "Oh my gosh." I couldn't believe I could actually smell its floral aroma. Giddy with the new revelation, I quickly sat up and sniffed to see if I could detect any other scents.

Normally, I'd have to be standing close to something before I could get a good whiff of it, but not today. Today, I could smell the odors coming from the kitchen—freshly brewed coffee, along with pancakes and bacon.

I rolled out of bed, pausing at the door when I remembered I was naked. Too excited to search for my nightgown or go back to my room for some clothes, I grabbed the nearest thing I could find, which happened to be Mitch's T-shirt. His scent still clung to the fabric, and inhaling the enticing aroma as I slipped it over my head had my cat purring.

I'd been able to smell Mitch before, but now that my allergies seemed to have cleared and weren't hindering my cat's sniffing abilities, his scent had grown even stronger, along with the urgent desire to find him.

When I arrived in the kitchen, I found him standing in front of the stove, flipping pancakes. He had his back to me, so I took a moment to admire the way his pale blue shirt and black slacks conformed perfectly to his body. I could tell by his damp hair that he'd recently showered, and after one whiff knew he'd used a body wash scented with sandalwood and a hint of musk.

I wasn't entirely sure how he'd react if I walked up behind him and slipped my arms around his waist, so I resisted the urge. "Good morning," I said as I padded across the cool tiles toward the kitchen island.

"Good morning to you too." He glanced over his shoulder, his dark gaze landing on the T-shirt I was wearing, his grin growing wider.

I leaned against the edge of the counter. "You should have woken me up. I would've been more than happy to help with breakfast."

"You looked so peaceful that I didn't have the heart to wake you. I have to go to work, but I was hoping to serve you breakfast in bed before I left." He nodded toward the tray on the counter containing a set of silverware and an empty plate. He'd even added a clear glass vase and filled it with a single wildflower.

No male had ever gone to this much trouble to impress me, and I felt guilty for ruining his surprise. "I could always go back to bed and pretend I'm sleeping."

After turning off the flame under the pan, he removed the last two cakes and dropped them on the plate containing the rest of the stack. "I have a better idea." He set the spatula aside, then lifted me by the waist and sat me on the counter.

Since I'd explored every inch of his body the previous night, I was familiar with the firm, rippling muscles on his shoulders I felt beneath my hands. What I hadn't expected was the electrical tingle pulsing along my fingertips or the exhilarating sense of recognition that surged through my body and increased the beat of my heart.

I gasped, afraid my difficulty breathing was the beginning of another panic attack.

"Hannah, are you okay?" Mitch rubbed my arms.

"I…" Leaning forward, I took another sniff of his neck to make sure I hadn't imagined what my senses were telling me was true. "You're…" I gasped some more.

His brow furrowed. "Hannah, you need to breathe. You're not making any sense." He cupped my cheek, sending more pleasant tingles across my skin.

Why I could feel the electrical charges now and not when he'd touched me before was baffling. Had my inability to scent properly been the reason I hadn't recognized him earlier? "The pills…allergies gone…can smell everything."

"That's a good thing, right?"

For me, it was a wonderful thing. How Mitch was going to feel about it was an uncertainty I dreaded. After a bob of my head and a hard swallow, I rasped, "You're my mate."

"What?" Shock flickered in his gaze, and the thumb caressing my cheek froze. "How is that possible?"

I wanted to ask him if he was kidding and point out that he knew darned well it was possible because his sister was mated to a bear. Instead, I held my tongue.

"Are you sure you're not mistaken?"

"Do you think I'd make something like this up?" I could accept him being as shocked as I was, but to ask me if I'd made a mistake over something this important was unacceptable. My temper flared, and I pushed against his chest until he moved so I could slide off the counter.

He snagged my wrist to keep me from leaving. "No, that's not what I'm saying at all. It's just that I never imagined…"

We were interrupted by the melodic chirp of his cell phone. By the third ring, he was growling and reaching around me to grab it off the counter. After glaring at whatever number had popped up, he roughly swiped his thumb across the screen. "This is Mitch." He'd kept the anger out of his voice, but his frown deepened the longer he listened. "Tell him to keep her calm, that I'll be there as fast as I can," he said to whoever was on the other end of the line.

After tucking his phone in his back pocket, he put his hands on my hips. "That was my afterhours service. There's been an emergency, and I need to go."

"I understand." I wanted to hear what he'd been about to say, but I wasn't about to keep him from a life-threatening situation.

"Can we talk about this when I get back?"

If Mitch believed me, it was unclear whether or not he

was happy about the revelation. "Yeah." I agreed, hoping that whatever he had to say didn't end with a rejection.

He gave me a worried glance, pressed a kiss to my forehead, then hurried from the room.

I'd lost my appetite and was no longer interested in the pancakes and bacon he'd made me for breakfast. I spent the next ten minutes putting the food in containers and cleaning up the kitchen before heading for my bedroom. At the moment, I couldn't deal with reminders of the wonderful night we'd shared and didn't bother stopping to grab my nightgown and underwear from Mitch's room.

When I reached my room, I plopped on the edge of the bed, wishing I hadn't told Mitch he was my mate. If I had it to do over again, I would take my time, not blurt it out without preparing him first. I thought about the bottle of pills sitting in the kitchen and wondered if my life might have been better if I'd never taken the darn things. At least when I left Colorado, I would've had great memories of the time he and I had spent together, not the pain tearing me apart, knowing there was a good chance my mate didn't want me.

CHAPTER EIGHT

MITCH

I was Hannah's mate.

At first, I was shocked, but once reality set in, I was elated. It was all I could think about during the drive to Gabe Miller's place. Gabe owned a nearby horse ranch that offered trail rides to visiting tourists. And because Berkley was a fantastic marketer who'd been able to work out a referral program with Gabe, both their businesses had benefitted financially.

The emergency I'd been called to assist with was a mare who was having trouble delivering her first foal. The little guy had been breech, the delivery difficult. If I hadn't arrived when I did there was a good chance Gabe would have lost the foal for sure, and possibly the mare.

Luckily, his arrival into the world had gone well, with mother and son doing fine. I stood near the wall inside the stall and watched the foal wobble on unsteady legs as he attempted to suckle from his mother. His chestnut coat was the same rich shade as hers, but the white patch covering his forehead was much larger.

"Thanks, Doc. I don't know what I would have done if

I'd lost both of them." Gabe clapped me on the shoulder and gave me a haggard smile, no doubt the result of worry and exhaustion.

A year ago, he'd installed cameras in the barn so he could monitor progress for any of his birthing mares. I had no idea if he used them, since I'd seen a rumpled sleeping bag and pillow on a portable cot in the walkway next to the row of stalls, a sure sign he'd spent most of the night in the building watching over her.

"I'm glad everything turned out okay." I grabbed a clean towel off a nearby stack and began wiping the drying blood off my arms.

Gabe glanced at the sullied condition of my clothes. "You're welcome to come inside and clean up, if you like."

I followed the direction of his gaze. The front of my shirt and the knees of my pants were covered in grime. No amount of scrubbing was going to make either of them presentable. "Thanks for the offer, but I think I'll head home and change before going into town."

Now that the emergency was over, my thoughts returned to Hannah. I'd called Noah on my way to Gabe's letting him know I'd be late and to make sure he didn't have a problem covering my appointments.

I was still kicking myself for the way I'd overreacted when she'd shared her news. Even worse was the guilt from seeing the pained expression on her face and knowing it was because she thought I was going to reject her.

If not for the untimely call from my afterhours service, I would have taken her back to bed and shown her, possibly for hours, how important she was to me. I needed to make things right with Hannah and was sure Noah wouldn't mind if I missed a couple more hours.

"Not a problem. I'll walk you out," Gabe said.

I picked my medical bag up off the straw covered ground as I walked out of the stall, then waited for Gabe to close the gate behind us. My truck was parked right outside the entrance to the barn, so we didn't have far to go.

"They both should be okay," I said as I set my bag behind the driver's seat, then hopped inside the vehicle. "But if you run into any problems, don't hesitate to call me."

"Will do, and thanks again."

I waited for Gabe to move away from my truck before backing up and heading down the drive that would take me back to the main highway. I had just turned left onto the two-lane road when the automatic link to my phone rang through the truck's speakers and Leah's name appeared in the small screen on the dashboard.

She was due to have the baby any day now, and I was concerned this might be the call. Not that I wasn't excited for my new niece or nephew to arrive, but I wasn't looking forward to any more interruptions that would keep me from getting home to Hannah. "Leah, is everything okay?"

"No, everything is not okay." Her tone grew anxious. It sounded like she was in a vehicle and had her phone on speaker.

"Is it time? Do you need me to take you to the hospital? Do you need me to find Bryson?" I was rambling worse than Hannah did when she was close to panicking.

"No, no, and no," she stated emphatically.

I tipped my head from side to side, trying to work out the tension in my neck. Lately, my sister's hormones ruled her emotions. I hoped I wasn't going to spend the next half hour placating her like I had the one and only time Bryson had teased her about looking like a basketball.

"Then what's wrong?"

"It's Hannah."

Hearing her name sent dread inching down my spine. "What about Hannah? Did something happen to her?"

"I... She..."

I heard some grumbling in the background, then Berkley's much calmer voice came on the line. "Hey,

Mitch, where are you?"

"I just left Gabe's place, and I'm on my way home."

"Good, that's good," she said.

Having lost all patience, I snarled, "Berkley, what aren't you telling me?"

"Leah got a call from Glenda, who got a call from one of her cousins, who told her the rangers got a report that there was a tiger running loose on your property."

"How the heck could anyone have seen Hannah in her animal form on my property? She's only been on one run since she started staying at my place, and that was a couple of days ago." Then I remembered what Hannah had said about hearing something else in the woods with us. My land was secluded, too far off the main road to access accidentally. Was it possible my assumption that we'd disturbed a small creature been wrong, that someone had been following us?

If that was the case, whoever had reported Hannah's cat had to have seen her before she'd shifted. Since she heard the noise after she'd transformed, there was a good chance the person was also a shifter. If they were human and were hanging around before and after her change, they would have freaked out and reported what they'd seen to the local newspaper, not the ranger station.

I couldn't shake the feeling that this was somehow personal, but no matter how much I analyzed what I knew, I couldn't figure out why.

"I don't know, but it's only a matter of time before someone shows up at your place to verify the information," Berkley said.

Hannah had no way of knowing about the new report or that someone might show up to try to trap her cat. "Did you call Hannah to let her know?" I asked, tempted to disconnect the line and make the call myself. If she stayed in the house and didn't shift when she went outside, it wouldn't matter if she got a visit from a ranger. But now that she no longer had any issues with allergies and could scent the way she was supposed to, I worried she might decide to go for a run without me.

"We've tried a few times, but she's not answering," Leah interrupted.

The pressure squeezing my chest tightened. I understood why my sister was so distraught. We were both worried that something might have happened to Hannah.

Going too fast on the winding road made traveling dangerous. Even so, I gripped the steering wheel harder and pushed the speed of my truck past what I considered safe.

I took the next curve a little faster than I should have and had to swerve back in my own lane to avoid hitting an oncoming car.

"We just left the lodge, but it sounds like you're a lot closer and should get there before we do," Berkley said.

"I'll see you there," I said, reaching for the Disconnect button on the dashboard

"Mitch, you need to be careful," Berkley warned before I could end the call. "There might be more going on than we know about."

It sounded as if she'd come to a similar conclusion. "That's what I'm afraid of."

CHAPTER NINE

HANNAH

Several hours had passed since Mitch left. I'd been sitting at the table in the kitchen nook and staring at the computer screen of my laptop for what seemed like forever, too upset to compose a single sentence.

Staying with him had been great for my writing. I had one chapter left to complete my book and thought after I'd taken a shower and gotten dressed that I'd be able to finish my work without any difficulty. I had been terribly wrong.

The longer he was gone, the more anxious my cat and I got. I had no idea what emergency he was taking care of, but since it was a workday, I was certain he'd be heading to his clinic in Ashbury once he was done.

My cat was in worse shape than I was. She was confused and didn't understand what had happened with Mitch. Her whining had grown more frequent, and so had her insistence that we track him down.

If Mitch had been a shifter, he would have recognized me as his mate from the moment we met, and I wouldn't be sitting here worrying about the outcome of the talk he wanted to have when he returned.

Since he was human and didn't have the same animalistic instincts I did, he wouldn't be experiencing the same overwhelming need to bond, to claim, to solidify our relationship for the rest of our lives.

I'd thought about calling Leah and asking her advice on the best way to deal with her brother. But I didn't think Mitch would appreciate me sharing the news with his sister. If he chose to refuse our connection, he might not want anyone else to be aware of the situation.

So far, attempting to write wasn't helping my frustration, and neither was sitting around waiting. Maybe going outside and getting some fresh air would take my mind off Mitch and stimulate my creative energies.

Now that I could scent everything vividly, it would be easier to keep track of where I was going. As far as I knew, the rangers had stopped searching for me, so I didn't see any reason why I couldn't go on a run without him, not if I kept it short and stayed on his property.

Even if my cat and I got distracted and strayed a little, I'd be able to find my way back to his house without any problems. Feeling minutely better, I stripped out of my clothes and draped them neatly over a kitchen chair. Once outside, I quickened my steps, then sprang from the end of the deck. By the time I hit the ground, I'd transformed into my cat.

I paused at the tree line and lifted my head, taking in the forest scents, a combination of damp leaves and pine from the surrounding trees. If I wasn't mistaken, a squirrel or two had recently been in the area.

Excited to find out what other scents I might discover, I headed into the woods. Fifteen minutes and several wildflower patches later, I caught the scent of a female wolf. The odor was fresh and belonged to Avery.

With a snarl, I perked my ears, the fur along my spine standing on end. My cat and I were ready to shred the wolf for daring to trespass near our mate's home. Once the animal side of my nature went into protective mode and started tracking the wolf, any control my human side had over her was lost.

The trail I followed wound through the trees and deeper into the forest. When the scent faded and I was about to give up, a wolf covered in dark brown fur the same shade as the hair of Avery's human half appeared in my path approximately ten yards away.

She raised her muzzle and released a challenging howl. I was determined to teach the female once and for all not to mess with my mate and accepted her challenge with a loud roar. As soon as I took after her, she disappeared into a nearby copse of trees.

She was fast and had a slight advantage when it came to dodging bushes. In areas where there were long stretches of ground, I was faster and able to close the distance. It didn't take me long to catch up with her.

When I was inches away from biting her flank, she jumped to the right. She bounded off a boulder and leaped over a brambly hedge and out of my reach. By the time I realized she was avoiding the opening to a long, round cylinder, it was too late.

No amount of backtracking could keep my paws from skidding inside and slamming against the hard surface at the other end.

The area was tight, and turning around was difficult. Before I could escape, a metal door swung shut, and I heard the sound of a lock clicking into place. I used all the strength I could muster and shoved the door with my shoulder, but couldn't get the metal panel to budge. I didn't handle small places well, and if the panel hadn't contained quarter-sized holes that let in air and enabled me to see outside, I would have panicked.

Avery had changed into her human form and was naked and standing a few feet away. I couldn't see or smell anyone else and figured she must have been the one who locked me inside. She stepped out of my view for a few seconds, and when she returned, she was carrying some clothes.

She set the pile on the nearby boulder, then sifted through the layers until she pulled out a cell phone.

"Evan had been right when he said this bear trap would work great for catching a tiger."

I didn't know who Evan was, but if she'd been discussing bear traps with him, there was a good chance he was a ranger.

"Cell service isn't great in this area, and I'm glad I decided to test it first before luring you out here."

With a sneer, she leaned closer, centered the lens on the back of the phone in one of the openings, then snapped a couple of pictures.

I blinked from the flash and snarled, then took a swipe, my paw making a loud thump.

Even though I couldn't reach her, Avery jumped back with a chuckle. She rapidly tapped on the lower half of her screen. "In case you were wondering, Evan's that new human ranger who recently started working at the station. I sent him a text telling him I was out hiking and found a tiger in his trap. I even included your picture for confirmation."

Forget leaving claw marks on her backside. If I ever got out of the trap, the maniacal wolf was going to endure some serious mauling.

After setting her phone on the boulder, she grabbed a pair of jeans off the stack and pulled them on. She'd gotten the zipper up and the button secured when a musical tune played on her phone, announcing an incoming text.

A quick glance at the screen had her grinning. "Perfect, he said he'll be here shortly to collect you." She picked up a shirt next, then tugged it over her head. "Since Evan doesn't know anything about our kind and is expecting to find a tiger when he arrives, I wouldn't advise shifting." She tucked her phone into her back pocket.

"Mitch is the only male who's ever turned me down, and with you out of the way, I'm certain I can change his mind."

Mitch was a great-looking male, and I could see why Avery was attracted to him. He was also intelligent, thoughtful, and caring. I didn't understand how she could only see him as a conquest and was convinced there was something seriously wrong with her.

If I thought it would do any good, I'd shift and tell her he was my mate. Since she'd gone to a lot of trouble to get me out of the way, I was pretty sure anything I had to say wasn't going to make any difference.

***

Avery's plan had been flawless, and I hated how easily I'd fallen for it. Shortly after she left, a human male wearing a tan uniform with a park service patch sewn to the sleeve, had arrived. When he'd removed his brimmed hat to lean forward and peer at me through the holes in the metal panel, I'd gotten a glimpse of the name badge pinned to his shirt pocket confirming that he was Evan Cleary, the ranger Avery had contacted.

After removing the brush he'd used to hide the wheels mounted beneath the platform, it didn't take him long to hook the trap up to the hitch on his truck and tow me to the nearest station.

I was already frustrated with myself, and being bounced around every time Evan drove over a rut in the road only made it worse. I'd spent the entire trip contemplating what I'd do if I ever saw Avery again—thoughts of shredding more than just her backside—and wishing I could see Mitch one more time. I didn't believe for one second Mitch would fall for Avery's ploy. It was the thought of never seeing my mate again that had more than one tear trickling along the fur on my face.

Evan finally stopped the vehicle near a building, the

front entrance constructed with an A-frame design. The wooden planks on the exterior of the structure had been stained a dark gray, the supporting posts near the front glass door covered with flat rocks in varying shades of white and light gray.

On the opposite side of where we'd parked, there was a sign for the Seneca Falls Ranger Station. Beyond that, all I could see was a panoramic view of a forest set against a mountain backdrop. Even if I could escape, which was highly unlikely, I had no idea where I was or how to get back to Mitch's place.

Evan appeared in my view with a cell phone pressed to his ear. "I'm waiting to hear back from my boss," he said to whoever was on the other end of the line as he paced back and forth a few feet away from me. "But more than likely, someone will have to put the animal down."

I cringed, wondering if the person he was sharing my fate with was Avery. I wouldn't put it past the evil she-wolf to call and verify her efforts to get rid of me had been successful. I could almost imagine her cooing that it was too bad, then snickering about my impending demise after she disconnected the call.

I heard the engine of another vehicle and watched a white truck with a long green stripe painted on the side, the word RANGER in capital letters centered in the portion running along the panel above the front tire.

"I've got to go," Evan said, then tucked his phone in his back pocket and waved at the male getting out of the truck. "Hey, Nash, how's it going?"

"It's going good." The male wore a similar uniform complete with a utility belt wrapped around his waist. "I heard you caught that tiger we've been getting reports about."

"Sure did." Evan stuck his chest out proudly as if he'd ensnared me without any help.

He stepped past Evan and stopped a couple of feet away from me. If I hadn't been able to tell Nash was a bear from his smell, his tall, broad frame and the way he lumbered toward me would have given it away.

"Good job," Nash said after he got a look at me. He was close enough to scent that I was a shifter, and his comment sounded more like a curse than a compliment for a job well done.

He scratched the light brown stubble on his chin while he stared speculatively at me. After a few seconds, his blue eyes widened, and he grinned.

"Before I forget." He faced Evan. "We got a report that some teenagers are skinny-dipping down at the public area near the falls. The chief wants you to go over there and check it out."

Evan frowned at me. "But what about the tiger?"

"I'll look after her until you get back." Nash gave Evan his back again so he could conceal the wink he gave me as he spoke.

"Here, you can take my truck." Nash reached into his pants pocket and pulled out a set of keys, then tossed them to Evan.

Evan caught them easily. "Okay. I guess I'll see you later then." He didn't sound happy about having to go, but reluctantly headed for Nash's truck.

"I'll be here." Nash crossed his arms, patiently waiting for Evan to leave.

Once the vehicle cleared the drive and disappeared from view, Nash gave the top of the cylinder a hard thwack. "Let's get you out of here."

I assumed getting me out of here meant freeing me, not driving me to another location, so I was disappointed when Nash started up the truck and began towing the trap onto the road. I had no idea where he was taking me, but from what I could see through the holes in the door, he was taking some back roads heading away from any sign of civilization and going farther into the wilderness area. And even farther away from Mitch.

It was hard to determine how long we traveled. Judging

by the location of the sun, I guessed it was late afternoon, maybe an hour or so before sunset. After driving along a narrow dirt road that wound closely between walls of ash and the occasional spruce tree, Nash parked the truck alongside a long porch that wrapped around a beautiful two-story home. The rustic design and wooden exterior of the house reminded me a lot of the lodge at the resort.

I heard a truck door open and close, followed by quick steps crunching on gravel before Nash appeared in front of me again. "You wait right here." He bent over so I could see his face. "I need to go in and talk to my brother real quick, and then I'll be right back to let you out."

Now that I had a mate, changing into my human form in front of another male wasn't going to happen. Otherwise, I'd have shifted and asked him where the heck he thought I was going to go, then yelled at him to open the door already. Instead, I chuffed out an exasperated groan, dropped onto my belly, and watched him take the porch steps two at a time before opening a screen door and disappearing inside.

I'd never had a problem with claustrophobia, but after being cooped up inside the trap for hours, and in desperate need of a bathroom, I was pretty sure it would be a long time before I entered another confined space. I might even start avoiding my walk-in closet back home.

A few seconds later, I heard doors slamming, loud grumbling, and roaring coming from inside the house. My irritation at Nash for leaving me caged quickly dissolved into a fearful panic. After imagining the worst possible scenarios, all of which ended badly for me, Nash finally reappeared on the porch, carrying a bundle of clothes in his arms.

He had to know I'd heard the noises and must have sensed my trepidation. He said, "Sorry about that. My brother Cooper gets real cantankerous if you wake him before he's ready to get up." He flashed me a charming grin, which I was certain he'd practiced on plenty of females. "You don't need to worry, though, because I fixed him some coffee, and he'll be good to go in no time."

Another male with light blond hair and facial features similar to Nash's stepped out onto the porch, appearing slightly annoyed. "I will, huh?" His deep voice rasped as if the growling I'd overheard had left his throat raw. He sat on the top step, his hands wrapped around a large ceramic mug.

"Keep drinking," Nash snapped as he set the pile of clothes on top of the trap. He released the latch securing the door and pulled it open so I could get out.

Excited to finally be free, I sprang out of the trap, putting some distance between the metal cage and me. I turned and stared at the brothers, waiting to see what they'd do next.

"I brought you something to wear." Nash patted the pile of clothes. "They belong to our sister so they won't smell like Cooper and me."

He must have picked up Mitch's scent, possibly knew he was my mate. Shifter males were extremely territorial when it came to their females. Mitch might be human, but it hadn't stopped Nash from being considerate and doing his best not to offend him. An act that earned him a few more favorable points.

"We'll wait for you inside." Nash headed for the porch, smacking Cooper in the shoulder with the back of his hand along the way.

"Right, we'll just…" Cooper tipped his head toward the house and got to his feet.

Being stuck out in the middle of nowhere with two bear shifters, one who'd initially been annoyed by my presence, didn't exactly relieve my fear or ease the pressure in my chest. It was less frightening than taking off on my own to find Mitch's house.

There was always the possibility of the pill wearing off and my allergies returning and leaving me in an even worse predicament. If Nash and Cooper had been chivalrous enough to consider providing me a female's clothes instead of a male's, I wanted to believe their intentions were honorable.

After waiting for them to go inside, I shifted back into my human form. I ignored the soreness in my muscles from being in a cramped position for so long and reached for the clothes. It appeared their sister had a similar build to her brothers. The T-shirt and pair of sweats I slipped into were several sizes too big. Not that I was going to complain.

Maybe after I explained what happened, they'd be willing to help me get back to Mitch. Reluctantly, and hoping I wasn't about to make my situation worse, I climbed the porch and knocked on the door before letting myself inside.

CHAPTER TEN

MITCH

Even though I was five minutes away from my house when I'd disconnected the call from Berkley and Leah, I tried to reach Hannah via her cell, and when that didn't work, I called the landline and still got nothing but voice mail.

There was always the possibility she was working and listening to music. If every nerve in my system wasn't screaming that something had happened to her, I might have believed it. Hannah was the type of person who faced life's difficulties head-on. No matter how upset she might be with me, I refused to believe she wouldn't answer my calls.

Once I reached the turnoff for my gravel driveway, it didn't take long to reach the house and bring the truck to a skidding stop next to Hannah's rental car. Knowing she hadn't left didn't ease the tension rippling through my system.

I hurried to the clinic door, freezing when I found it partially open. All my clients knew I worked in town during the week, and I was in the habit of locking the door whenever I was gone.

The possibility of Hannah using the exit, then forgetting to close the door was slim. There were no signs the lock had been forced, yet it didn't stop me from worrying that someone had gotten inside.

I heard growling coming from somewhere inside the house. If the threat to Hannah was another shifter as I'd expected, fighting with my bare hands wasn't going to do any good. Not when claws and fangs were involved.

I hurried back to the truck to retrieve my dart gun, then quietly eased the door the rest of the way open. The farther I moved along the hallway, the louder the growling got, and the more my heart raced.

I made it as far as the living room when the low, guttural sounds turned into an unfamiliar female's voice. "Where is Hannah?"

If it was Hannah who was in trouble, then why would someone be asking where she was? Keeping the gun leveled in front of me, I turned the corner into the living room and found a female I'd never seen before straddling Avery's chest and pinning her to the hardwood floor. The hood of her navy blue jacket had slipped to the back of her head, exposing obsidian hair sprinkled with silvery-blue streaks.

The color looked too natural to be something created in a salon, and I suspected she might be a shifter, though what kind, I had no idea.

"That's what I'd like to know," I said, taking a few steps closer. After the way both females had jerked their heads and were glaring at me, I was afraid I might get torn to shreds, and decided to keep my distance and the gun aimed in their direction.

The female with unusual hair tightened the grip she had on the front of Avery's shirt and said, "Whoa, don't shoot. I'm one of the good guys."

"Mitch, thank goodness you're here." Avery squirmed but couldn't dislodge the other female. "Please make her get off me."

"Not until I get some answers." Trusting Avery or believing anything she had to say wasn't going to happen. I had no reason to trust the stranger either, but as long as she continued to keep Avery constrained, I was willing to hear what she had to say.

"Mitch, I…"

"Be quiet, Avery," I interrupted. "I want to hear what she has to say." I wiggled the gun in the stranger's direction. "Let's start with who you are, what happened to Hannah, and what you're doing in my house."

She pushed her hood the rest of the way off her head. "My name is Sydney Jamison, and I'm Hannah's best friend."

Footsteps from the hallway preceded my sister shouting my name in a distressed voice.

"Leah, I'm in here," I called without taking my eyes off the females.

"What's going on?" Berkley reached me first, took one look at the scene in front of me, and snarled, "Avery. I should have known."

"Berkley, it's not what you think," Avery said.

"Oh, I'm pretty sure it is." Berkley fisted her hands against her thighs.

"What's Avery doing here?" Leah glared at the two females as she waddled into the room. "Wait a minute." She pointed at Sydney. "You're the person who was following us, the one who ran into the light pole."

Sydney blushed. "Not one of my better moments, but yes."

"You're not a stalker, are you?" Leah asked.

"No, I'm a mountain guide." Sydney huffed at the insult.

"That doesn't explain what you're doing in my brother's house." Leah eased herself onto the sofa and began rubbing her belly. It seemed my sister wanted to be comfortable now that she'd taken over the interrogation.

"I'm Hannah's friend Sydney. I finished my last job early, and when I got her message telling me about her trip here, I decided to surprise her. Only, when I arrived at her cabin, it was empty." She adjusted her weight when Avery tried to free herself again.

"I was hanging out in the reception area at the lodge, hoping to find out where she'd gone, when I overheard you two"— Sydney wiggled her finger between Leah and Berkley—"talking about picking her up and taking her into town. So I followed you."

I remembered Hannah saying she hadn't gotten a good look at the person following us. I was certain if she'd recognized her best friend, she would've said something. "Why all the mystery? Why not let Hannah know you'd arrived?"

Sydney smiled. "Mostly because of the way she was looking at you when you were coming out of the restaurant. Hannah's never acted that way around a male before, and I didn't want to get in the way if it turned out to be something romantic."

"If you didn't want her to know you were in town, how did you end up being here today?" I asked, not totally satisfied with her answer.

"I was keeping an eye on her because her ca...I mean she has a tendency to get into trouble. It's not her fault." Sydney's scowl reflected her uncertainty.

I had to give her credit for wanting to protect Hannah's secrets. Both of which—Hannah being a shifter and having an allergy issue—Sydney probably wasn't aware I already knew.

"Yes, I know."

"Anyway..." Sidney shot a glare in Avery's direction. "That's how I caught her breaking into your house and taking Hannah's stuff." She glanced behind her where a couple of Hannah's suitcases were sitting on the floor. They were partially hidden by my recliner; otherwise, I might have noticed them sooner.

I lowered my gun and placed it on the end table near the sofa, confident Berkley was more than capable of taking over if things got out of hand. I walked over to Sydney and offered to help her up. "You can let Avery go now. I don't think she's going anywhere."

Sydney sniffed the air as soon as she was standing. "I was right about you and Hannah. I can smell her all over you." She grinned, her slate-gray eyes sparkling as she paused to catch another whiff. "And you recently had sex."

I wasn't sure what was more embarrassing, the fact that she could tell what Hannah and I had been doing simply by smelling, or that she'd announced it to everyone in the room. And if she could tell, it meant my shifter friends could too. As much as I yearned to know everything I could about their kind, I could have gone my whole life not knowing that particular tidbit.

"That's because I'm Hannah's mate," I blurted out before any of the other females, more specifically my sister, could make a chastising remark.

Berkley and Leah didn't seem surprised by the revelation, but Sydney seemed rather elated. "You are. That's awesome." Her wide grin dimpled her cheeks.

"What?" Avery jumped to her feet. "No, that's not possible!"

"Yes, it is." I blew out an exasperated sigh. "Now can we please get back to finding out what happened to Hannah?"

Avery pursed her lips and hugged her chest tightly, refusing to speak.

Sydney furrowed her brow. "That's what I was trying to do before you all got here, but I couldn't get her to talk."

Rushed footsteps sounded in the hallway, drawing everyone's attention. Nick entered the room holding Mandy's hand, making sure that she stayed behind him and well protected.

He was dressed in an old pair of sweats and a worn T-shirt and wasn't wearing any shoes. I assumed he must've been at home working in his woodwork shop before coming to my place. We all knew he preferred to go barefoot unless he was going to be around humans.

"Did you guys find Hannah?" Mandy asked as she moved to stand beside her mate.

"Not yet." Berkley glanced expectantly behind the new arrivals. "Reese and Jac?" She asked Mandy with a raised brow.

"They wanted to come too, but thought someone should stay behind and take care of things at the lodge."

Nick sniffed the air the same way Sydney had, then glanced at me and grinned. "Mitch, congrats. Mandy told me you found your mate."

It was more likely that Berkley had already figured it out, then told Mandy, who in turn told Nick.

"Thanks, but she's not here, and we're pretty sure Avery knows what happened to her," I said.

Berkley flicked her right wrist, her nails extending into sharp claws. "I was looking forward to extracting the information from her myself, but now that you're here, I'm sure we can get the answers a lot faster."

Avery shuddered and took a few steps backward. "Berkley, you can't be serious. His wolf will kill me."

Nick was part wild wolf. In the shifter world, they had a reputation for being antisocial loners whose animals couldn't always be controlled and sometimes turned feral.

Mandy smiled proudly at her mate. "You should've thought of that before you messed with a member of our family."

"Maybe you should take her outside," Leah said. "It's difficult to scrub the blood out of the cracks on a hardwood floor."

"It would definitely make getting rid of the body parts a lot easier," Berkley added.

Sydney had no way of knowing the female's comments

were meant to intimidate, to get Avery to talk. Shock flickered in the glance she gave Berkley and my sister, as if she truly believed their intentions.

"Sounds good to me." Nick grabbed Avery's arm and pulled her toward the sliding glass doors leading out to the deck. It only took one of his deep, hair-raising growls to stop her from struggling.

"Mind if I come along? I asked.

"Are you sure you want to watch?" Nick asked me.

"I'm not squeamish, and I'll do whatever it takes to get Hannah back."

Avery braced her hand against the doorframe to keep Nick from dragging her outside. "Fine, stop. I'll tell you whatever you want to know." She hastened away from Nick as soon as he released her.

"Tell me where Hannah is, and know that if she is harmed in anyway, I will gladly turn you over to Nick's wolf." I preferred saving lives, but wouldn't care about sparing Avery's if I lost Hannah.

Avery swallowed hard. "I waited for her to go for a run, then lured her tiger into one of those cylindrical bear traps, then called Evan at the ranger's station and told him where he could find her."

After hearing what Avery had done and knowing how scared Hannah must be, I was tempted to change my mind about Nick taking her outside.

Berkley shook her head in disgust and pulled her cell out of her skirt pocket. "I'll call Reese, tell him what we found out, and have him contact his friend over at the ranger station." She walked into the kitchen for a little privacy.

Sydney gazed at the suitcases. "Why were you taking Hannah's things?"

"I knew Mitch would be working in town and wanted to make it look like she'd left him," Avery's tone lacked any remorse.

"Why would you do something so maniacal?" Leah

snapped.

"With Hannah gone, I knew I could convince him he'd be better off with me." Avery jutted her chin, her self-confidence never wavering.

"What about finding your own mate?" Mandy slipped an arm around Nick's waist.

Avery wrinkled her nose, then glared at everyone in the room. "You all know that not everyone finds their mate." Her disgust quickly changed into one of boredom. "Most of the available shifter males I know wanted to wait for their mates, and I got tired of waiting for mine."

"But why me?" From what I'd observed, the female never lacked male attention.

"I thought you'd make a worthy mate since I couldn't seduce you as easily as I could the other human males in town. I found you even more appealing after seeing the way you acted with Hannah at the restaurant."

Sydney shook her head in disgust. "Unbelievable."

Berkley walked back into the room, concern creasing her brow. "Reese confirmed that Evan did pick up the trap and took Hannah to the station."

"Then why don't you look happy about it?" I asked.

"Because not long afterward, Nash Bradshaw showed up and drove off with Hannah still inside the trap."

"Oh, that's not good." Leah winced and rubbed her belly. "Sorry, mild contraction, nothing to worry about." She blew out a deep breath. "According to Glenda, the Bradshaw brothers are distant relatives and a little wild."

"Great." I gripped my nape. "You're saying my mate has been abducted by bears?"

"It looks that way." Berkley patted my arm. "There is good news."

I was finding it difficult to believe. "Yeah, which is?"

"Reese's friend was able to activate the truck's GPS, and it showed the vehicle heading in the direction of Nash's home."

"Please tell me he gave you an address?" I pulled the

truck keys out of my pocket, anxious to go after Hannah.

"What are we going to do with her?" Sydney hitched her thumb at Avery.

"I have an idea." I'd considered taking her with us, but I didn't want her anywhere near Hannah again. I picked up the gun and shot Avery in the thigh with a dart. Watching her hit the floor with a thud made me feel a little better, and would be the only satisfaction I'd get until I had Hannah safely wrapped in my arms.

"We can worry about taking her to the sheriff's office in Hanover when we get back. Until then, we can lock her in one of the kennels I use for overnight patients in the clinic."

"Sounds like a good plan to me." Nick chuckled, then heaved Avery over his shoulder and followed me to the back of the house. By the time Nick and I were done, everyone else was outside waiting for us by the vehicles.

I'd assumed my sister would ride back to the lodge with Berkley. Instead, she headed for my truck. "Leah, where do you think you're going?"

"Hannah is your mate, which means she's family." She pulled the passenger door open. "I'm going with you."

"I don't think that's a good idea. We have no idea what we're going to run into out there." I didn't want to wrestle a pregnant woman, but I would if I had to.

She snorted and grabbed the bar above the door, then stepped on the side rail so she could hoist herself into the passenger seat. I glanced at Berkley hoping for some support and got a shrug before she climbed in the back seat with Sydney.

I scrubbed my hand along my face. At this rate, I wasn't going to live long enough to claim Hannah. Bryson was going to kill me long before I got the chance.

CHAPTER ELEVEN

MITCH

The address and driving directions Berkley had gotten from Reese for the Bradshaws' property hadn't exactly been accurate. She'd had to plug the information into the GPS app on her phone before we were able to find the correct turnoff leading to their home. It was late in the afternoon with sunset less than forty-five minutes away by the time I pulled in front of their house. Nick and Mandy had followed us in their vehicle and parked behind us on the gravel driveway.

Seeing the white forest service truck with a bear trap attached to the rear hitch made what Avery had told us she'd done to Hannah enrage me even more. All I could think about was finding my mate, making sure she was safe, and holding her in my arms. I jumped out of the truck and rushed to glimpse inside the trap. After finding it empty, I ignored Berkley's warning to wait and climbed the porch steps.

I was beyond politely knocking. I had my hand on the screen door, ready to yank it open when Nick said my name. He clapped a reassuring hand on my shoulder to let me know he was there to support me, and probably also to keep me from doing something stupid. Like provoking some bear shifters by entering their territory without an invitation.

I gave him a brief nod, then glanced behind me to see Berkley and Mandy helping Leah out of the truck. I would have preferred my sister stay inside the vehicle where she'd be safe, but knew arguing would be useless. I also didn't want to waste any more time getting to Hannah.

"Did you hear that?" Sydney had also joined us and tilted her head, her ears perked. I strained to listen and heard muffled voices coming from outside, somewhere near the side of the house.

"This way," I said, heading toward another set of stairs on the other end of the wraparound porch, with Sydney and Nick trailing close behind me.

"That ought to do it," I heard a male say as I turned the corner leading to the back of the house. A few more steps, and I froze at the sight I found. Hannah was lying on the ground, unmoving. A male I assumed had to be one of the Bradshaw brothers squatted next to her. Even in his lowered position, it was easy to tell from the shirt clinging to his broad chest that the male was tall, with a massive build. I couldn't see Hannah's face, but there was blood on one of the male's hands and a large patch covering a portion of Hannah's oversized shirt.

Within seconds, I was reliving the nightmares of not being able to save Hannah. With a rush of adrenaline and giving no thought to my own safety, I raced toward the male. "Get away from her!" I shouted, then barreled into him. Stunned by my attack, the male didn't have time to react and ended up on his back with me fisting his shirt and straddling his chest.

"Nash, don't you dare hurt him," Hannah cried, rolling to her feet and hurrying toward me.

Nash's disbelieving frown deepened. "Hurt him? But I'm the one…"

"Hannah, are you okay?" I climbed off Nash and hurried to pull her into my arms.

"Of course, I'm all right." She tipped her head back and smiled, her green eyes sparkling. "We were…"

"Doing a reenactment," Sydney said with a grin as she approached, arms raised expectantly.

"Syd, what are you doing here?" Hannah pulled away from me and went to hug her friend.

"My tour ended early, and when I heard your message, I thought I'd join you in case you needed help staying out of trouble. It seems I was right, but it turns out to have been a good thing." Sydney grinned at me.

"Well, I'm glad to see you." Hannah squeezed Sydney one more time, her gaze taking in my friends as well. "All of you."

A door on the side of the house opened, and another male who looked like he was related to the one I'd knocked to the ground walked out the side entrance. He was fidgeting with a digital camera strapped around his neck. "What's going on here?" he said when he looked up and saw my friends and me. His gaze shot to Nash, who was rubbing his back as he got to his feet. "And what the hell did you do to my brother?"

"Cooper." Hannah stepped defensively in front of me. "This is Mitch and our friends from the lodge."

It troubled me that she hadn't introduced me as her mate, a reminder that things were still unsettled between us. I wrapped an arm around her waist and pulled her back against my chest.

Berkley shot Nash and Cooper the same sisterly glare I'd seen her use on her own brothers. "Why didn't you two call to let Mitch know where Hannah was and that she was safe?"

"I wouldn't mind hearing the answer to that myself." Leah had taken a seat in a cushioned patio chair not far from where Nick and Mandy were standing.

"It's not their fault." Hannah nervously glanced around

the group. "My cell phone is back at Mitch's place, and I couldn't remember any of his numbers."

"Besides, we were going to bring her home as soon as we were finished taking our pictures," Cooper said.

"Honest," Nash added.

"Pictures for what?" I asked.

Hannah bit her lower lip as she dropped her head to the side to look up at me. "It turns out the guys are fans. We got to talking about how I came up with ideas for my scenes, which led to my process, which led to me sharing my recipe, which led to this." She pulled her shirt out and glanced at the red spot she'd created with her fake blood.

This was the second time in the last day her special recipe had caused me undue anxiety. Either I would need to stop overreacting, or maybe I could convince her to use a different color. Maybe a nice shade of green to match her eyes.

"I promised to let them help me do a reenactment in return for saving my life."

A call would have relieved my stress, but I couldn't fault her for wanting to repay the brothers. "Hannah means the world to me, so thank you for looking after my mate."

Hannah jerked her head in my direction. "Your mate? Really?" She turned in my arms.

"Absolutely." I cupped the side of her face, wiping a smudge of dried "blood" off her cheek with my thumb.

She appeared confused, yet hopeful. "But this morning…"

"I was under the impression that shifters recognized their mates immediately. Since you hadn't said anything even while we were…" I stopped myself when I caught Nash and Cooper grinning. "Anyway, up until this morning, I knew you'd be leaving and was doing my best not to get my hopes up. That's why I asked if you were mistaken, not because I didn't want you."

"Mitch," Leah interrupted. "Do you suppose you could

hurry and get to the part where you tell her you love her?"

I glared at my sister. Hormone imbalance or not, I wasn't going to rush this moment with Hannah. As it was, I'd hoped to do this while we were alone so I could show her how I felt, not give her a verbal explanation in front of our friends. "Would you mind giving me a couple more minutes, *please*?"

"We don't have the time, because my water just broke." Leah glanced at the wet spot forming on her pants. "Someone needs to take me to the hospital and call Bryson."

CHAPTER TWELVE

MITCH

The hospital in Hanover had a special floor designated for treating shifters, one very few humans knew anything about. Over the course of Leah's pregnancy, I'd learned quite a bit about what to expect. Other than a shorter gestation period—usually around seven months—and a quicker delivery time, birthing was no different than it was for humans.

Bryson had arrived shortly after we did, looking excited yet pale. He hadn't been happy when I'd called and told him Leah had accompanied us to the Bradshaw residence. He'd muttered something about crazy relatives before ending the call with a growl. I was afraid he'd be worse by the time he arrived at the hospital, and was glad when one of the nurses ushered him into the private delivery room with Leah.

Berkley was currently on the phone chatting with Jac. She'd already talked to Preston and Reese to give them an update. Hannah and I were glad when she'd told us the males had volunteered to go by my house and collect Avery so we wouldn't have to deal with her once we got home.

Nick had miraculously found some shoes during the drive. No doubt he kept the pair of slip-ons in his truck for emergencies. It was common knowledge within our group that he didn't do well around crowds, mostly because of his wolf. After catching him glancing at the exit as if he wanted to bolt, Mandy planted herself on his lap to keep him distracted.

I had no idea why the Bradshaw brothers thought they needed to be here. Distant relatives of Bryson's or not, I'd been informed by Leah that they were family and were welcome to come along. I was pretty sure Cooper made the trip because of his interest in Sydney. Though it wasn't clear why the two of them had spent the last half hour sitting on opposite sides of the waiting room, glaring at each other.

I got the impression Nash didn't want to miss out on any excitement and came along so he could flirt with the female staff. At the moment, he was leaning on the counter of the nurse's station, charming a young blonde who giggled every now and then at something he'd said.

Ryder, the oldest of the three brothers, hadn't said much after showing up with Bryson. He was still wearing his ranger uniform, back braced against a wall with his arms crossed, his expression somber. The few times I'd caught him glancing in Nash's direction, he was shaking his head.

The only reason Bryson's parents hadn't shown up to wait for their grandchild to be born was because they'd been on their way to the airport in Denver to pick up Dora. They wouldn't be getting back until late, but things were certain to be a lot livelier tomorrow after I introduced Hannah to my mother.

"Are you nervous?" Hannah was sitting in the seat next to me, tucked under my arm with her head resting on my shoulder.

I pulled her closer. "No, I'm actually looking forward

to being an uncle."

She groaned and pursed her lips. "I meant about you and me."

"Totally terrified." I laughed.

She straightened and smacked my chest. "I'm serious."

"I know you are." I placed my hand over hers. Shifters had exceptional hearing, and I leaned closer so only she could hear me. "I have been waiting my whole life for you." I kissed her forehead. "Now that I know you're my mate, I can't wait to get you home."

Bryson burst through the door he'd disappeared behind earlier, his grin the widest I'd ever seen it. "I'm a father."

"Bryson, wait," I called when he turned to leave again. No one in our group seemed surprised that the male had reverted back to saying only what he thought was necessary. I at least wanted to know if I had a new niece or nephew. "Is it a boy or a girl?"

"Megan is a girl." It was a beautiful name, and I couldn't wait to find out if she looked like her mother.

The nurse who had come up behind Bryson jumped out of his way to keep from being knocked over. She addressed us as soon as he disappeared down the corridor. "Baby and mom are doing fine, but they're resting, so you'll all have to come back tomorrow during regular visiting hours to see them."

The room filled with disappointed moans. I was surprised we'd been allowed to stay this long. Thanks to Berkley and her connections, no one had asked us to leave. I had no doubt we'd all be back first thing in the morning to get a glimpse of the newest addition to our family.

I got to my feet and pulled Hannah with me. "You'll have to excuse us," I said to the group, then grabbed Hannah around the waist and tossed her over my shoulder.

She squealed and grabbed the back of my shirt. "What do you think you're doing?"

"Taking my mate home so I can claim her." I wrapped my arms around her legs to keep her in place.

"And I have it on good authority that this is part of the ritual." Nick was notorious for carting Mandy off in a similar method. I gave him a conspiratorial wink on my way to the exit, my mind already filling with the numerous ways I planned to make my bond with Hannah permanent.

ABOUT THE AUTHOR

Rayna Tyler is an author of paranormal and sci-fi romance. She loves writing about strong sexy heroes and the sassy heroines who turn their lives upside down. Whether it's in outer space or in a supernatural world here on Earth, there's always a story filled with adventure.

Printed in Great Britain
by Amazon

76830199R00061